THE
PLEASURE
OF HIS
COMPANY

LINDSAY EVANS

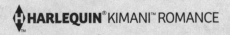

Recycling programs
for this product may
not exist in your area.

ISBN-13: 978-0-373-86510-9

The Pleasure of His Company

Copyright © 2017 by Lindsay Evans

For questions and comments about the quality of this book please contact us
at CustomerService@Harlequin.com.

Printed in U.S.A.

www.Harlequin.com

Lindsay Evans was born in Jamaica and currently lives and writes in Atlanta, Georgia, where she's constantly on the hunt for inspiration, club in hand. She loves good food and romance and would happily travel to the ends of the earth for both. Find out more at www.lindsayevanswrites.com.

Books by Lindsay Evans

Harlequin Kimani Romance

Pleasure Under the Sun
Sultry Pleasure
Snowy Mountain Nights
Affair of Pleasure
Untamed Love
Bare Pleasures
The Pleasure of His Company

Visit the Author Profile page
at Harlequin.com for more titles.

To my readers:
without you, none of this would be possible. Thank you!

Chapter 1

A beautiful man flying above the sea and into the sky wasn't something Adah saw every day. From the beach, she drew a breath and felt her whole body flush as the man sailed across the bright blue water and even closer to her. Thin board shorts and a T-shirt clung to his hard body, the wet material of both outlining every ridge of muscle and plane of skin. He was absolutely gorgeous, and she wasn't the only one looking.

"Damn, he is fine!" A woman down the beach said the words loudly enough to get chuckles of agreement from others nearby, pointing her camera up. Adah resisted the urge to reach for her phone to take a photo; instead she raised her hand above her eyes to shield her face from the Aruban sun burning brightly, even through her sunglasses.

They called it kite surfing. She knew that much from the signs on the event stage she'd seen on her walk from the hotel. And if the reaction of the audience was anything to go by, this gentleman was very good at it. Earlier she'd walked up in time to see him getting ready on the beach. He'd grabbed the edges of some sort of parachute, slipped his bare feet into slots on top of the board and then skated across the water, the bright-blue-and-white material of his parachute snapping in the breeze.

Fine was right.

Adah took off her sunglasses and watched him float across the water and just under the sky, turning somersaults while the audience cheered and called out what she assumed was his name. The announcer of the Hi-Winds Tournament shouted his praise as the man turned yet another flip and landed firmly on both feet on the deep blue sea. Then he was off, flying away from the shore and giving another kiter a turn in front of the rapt audience.

"Did you see that butt?" One of the bikini-clad girls near Adah said to her friend while they both giggled over their bottles of beer.

Her words made Adah blush and turn away from the water. She wasn't much better than this girl, ogling the man just because she was looking for a source of distraction from her own problems. But that awareness didn't stop her from sending one last lingering look across the water to where the man was making a loop in the sky and flying back toward the edge of the beach.

Although watching him made her feel vaguely uncomfortable in her own body, tingly and aware of long-ignored wants, it also felt good to be distracted from thoughts of the phone call she'd had with her mother earlier that morning.

"You have to make up your mind about this marriage, Adah," her mother had said. "You've already said yes to this. Just make it official so we can start making concrete plans for the wedding. Let's at least agree on a date."

A date to join her life with another person's to help save the family business.

Her mother made it sound so simple. Confirm the day for the arranged marriage she'd agreed to when she was a junior in college, depressed from a recent breakup and fixated on the idea that she'd never find a man to love her the way her father loved her mother. Back then she'd been convinced they didn't make men like her father anymore—honest, romantic, ride or die. To her, males of the species were all *boys* and would mature only enough to treat a woman like another notch on their bedposts.

And now, at twenty-six, she was still single but less sure she was willing to give up any chance at passion and love to rescue the family business. That was what she *should* be willing to do. That was what her twin sister, Zoe, would probably have done. But what-ifs didn't matter. Zoe was dead. It was Adah's responsibility to step up.

Seawater rushed over her sandaled toes, and she hissed at the coolness of it. Without realizing it, she'd walked to the edge of the sand and into the waves. Adah skittered back, annoyed with herself for getting water on the expensive leather sandals that had been a gift from her best friend. She should have just worn her plastic Old Navy flip-flops.

Farther up the beach, the tournament continued. Adah was out of the way of the kiters assembling on the beach as their competitors helped them get into their complicated-looking gear. It was a beautiful display of cooperation and partnership.

"You going to walk into the water with your clothes on?"

She jerked her attention from the beach only to find herself immersed in seductive brown eyes. It was the man who had danced in the air above the waves. Up close he was a gorgeous thing. Tall and sun-browned, white teeth blazing in his handsome face, radiating as much heat as the sun overhead. He still wore his loose T-shirt and board shorts, both wet from his time in the water. Mirrored sunglasses hung from the neck of his shirt.

"Things aren't that bad for me yet," she managed past a tight throat. Why was he talking to her? Men this good-looking never went out of their way to engage her in conversation.

"That's looking on the positive side." He grinned again, then came close. "I'm Kingsley."

His mouth was a firm curve, the top lip slightly smaller than the lower, both glistening with some sort of sunscreen or lip balm. Adah licked her own lips, which tasted like cherry Carmex, and imagined his tasted the same.

"Pleased to meet you." She almost slapped herself on the forehead at the inanity of her reply. But she felt completely undone. Her heart beat quickly in her chest, and her tongue felt too heavy for her to speak.

"A mystery woman, then?"

She shook her head but didn't correct him. Better he thought she was being mysterious and coy than an idiot who lost all her cool points just because a hot guy smiled at her. He shoved his hands in his pockets, seemingly unbothered.

"I saw you earlier," he said, eyes moving quickly over her body in a way that was both appraising and appreciative. "I had to come by and say hello."

"You saw me when you were in the air? You must have really good eyesight."

"That's not the only thing good about me," he said. Then he laughed at his own bad joke. "I'm sorry," he said as the last of his laughter faded. "I'm really not that corny."

"Somehow I have my doubts." But he still managed to charm her anyway. Adah felt herself responding to more than just his physical appeal. His eyes were warm with humor and his above-average height made her feel secure instead of intimidated. She could easily imagine cuddling into his big body after sex, her body humming with contentment as he stroked the length of her back in a soothing rhythm.

But there was something destructive in that. Something that made Adah's stomach clench in warning. This wasn't what she'd come to Aruba for.

As if he'd read her mind, Kingsley's look became downright seductive. Heavy-lashed eyes and an intimate smile like the door opening to a softly lit bedroom.

"Would you like to have a drink with me sometime?" he asked.

Adah automatically shook her head although she desperately wanted to say yes.

I'm in a situation. The words from the old Erykah Badu song rang ridiculously in her ear. That was one way to put it. And that was even assuming he felt even a little of what was thrumming over her skin. Pure and undiluted attraction. Lust and the urge to smile back at him just to see those compelling brown eyes narrow even more from his grin, the corners crinkling in the simple pleasure of sharing space with someone attractive. She couldn't remember the last time someone's mere presence had made her want to stay in his company and enjoy the ease of his smile, the comfort of his body. Because it was undoubtedly desire. It coursed through her veins just from looking at him. His undivided attention felt like hands running over her bare skin.

"I can't," she finally said. Not *I don't want to*.

And he seemed absolutely aware of the difference, judging from the way he looked at her, hungry and with the knowledge that the thing he wanted was within reach.

"I…uh… I have to go. Hope you win…whatever it is you're going after." She gestured to the kites still in the air, the stage and the people watching the action from the beach.

"And still no gift of your beautiful name?"

She shook her head again, this time not hiding her smile. "My name doesn't matter."

"I disagree." He paused, his gaze amused and thoughtful. "I have to call you something in my dreams."

Adah rolled her eyes. *Cute and corny.* "Call me whatever you like."

"I think I'll call you Doe Eyes." Then he grinned at her, apparently pleased with himself.

She shook her head a third time. "It was nice to meet you."

"It'll be even nicer to see you again," Kingsley said. Before she could tell him the island wasn't small enough for them to run into each other without agreeing to a time and place, his smile flashed again. "This won't be the last time," he said. The sand pulled at her sandals, and she stumbled, blushing as she righted herself under his amused regard. "Be careful until I see you again," he said with another quick scan up and down her body.

When he turned and walked away, she shamelessly watched him, the loose fit of the drying shirt over his muscled back and the shift of his butt in the long shorts. She bit her lip. There was joy in Kingsley. She thought about what sex would be like with him—undeniably hot, uninhibited—and knew there would be a spontaneous delight about the encounter, a pleasure at living and breathing and being able to gulp deeply from the cup of life. He was a man worth knowing. And touching.

"I know you're looking," he called over his shoulder without turning around. Laughter threaded through his voice. The sound of it should have made Adah blush and look away like a thief caught with her hands in the cookie jar, but she only grinned and kept looking until she could no longer make out the finer details of his physique.

She was still smiling when she walked across the sand and through the beachfront entrance of her hotel. The lavish hotel, though stretching the limits of her budget, was one she was glad to have found. Her room overlooked the water, the entire reason for her visit to an island in the Caribbean.

"Welcome back, Ms. Palmer-Mitchell." The woman at the front desk spared a smile for Adah as she looked up from her computer screen.

"Thank you."

"There's a visitor here for you. She's already in her own room, which she requested next to yours."

Adah stopped. "A visitor?" A bad feeling made

her footsteps stutter. The leftover warmth from the encounter with Kingsley leached from her. She shivered.

"Yes. She arrived about thirty minutes ago."

Adah had been walking the island for nearly two hours, trying to clear her mind and find a solution to the unsettled feeling that had yanked her out of her sleep nearly every night for the past six months. She was desperate for a good night's sleep.

Adah pressed her lips closed and sucked them between her teeth. "All right, thank you so much for letting me know."

After wishing the woman a good morning, she crossed the tiled lobby, each step feeling heavier than the last as she imagined who was waiting for her upstairs. She knew only one person with the means and motive to come to Aruba and turn her peace upside down. When the elevator doors slid open on her floor, there was someone waiting to get on it. The woman, elegant in white linen with her iron-gray hair on top of her head in a simple French twist, smiled at her in equal parts relief and triumph. Adah released a quiet breath.

"Hello, Mother."

Chapter 2

"Surprise, darling!" Thandie Palmer-Mitchell rebounded beautifully from the surprise of seeing Adah in the elevator.

Adah wished she could say the same for herself. Her suspicion had turned into grim certainty when the elevator doors opened on her floor. She felt scattered to the four winds at the sight of her mother, gorgeously styled and smiling in the last place Adah wanted her to be.

"Are you heading down?"

"Not anymore, now that you're here," her mother said.

Of course not. What she hoped was a smile spasmed across Adah's face. "Okay. My room or yours?"

"Yours, of course. You must want to shower and get cleaned up after being out there in the heat." Her mother fanned her face with her slender clutch purse as she stepped back to let Adah off the elevator. "After ten minutes out there, it felt like my skin was covered with sand and sweat."

She fell in step with Adah down the wide and well-lit hallway toward the small room Adah had booked. Adah cringed, suddenly remembering her mess. Although she'd been in Aruba for only a day, most of the contents of her suitcase were already spread all over the room, a tendency toward untidiness she carried over from how she treated her space at home. The common areas were orderly and almost obsessively neat, but her bedroom and bathroom were booby-trapped with piles of clothes, books and makeup in danger of falling over.

She wasn't dirty, Adah often reassured herself, just disorganized. Her habit of just stuffing her rolled travel clothes into her suitcase in no discernible pattern meant she often had to dig to the bottom of her luggage to find the exact thing she needed. Then after all that searching, who wanted to repack everything? There was just no point.

Her mother was the complete opposite. She used packing cubes, elegant and expensive, that she carefully arranged before each trip. Underwear in one cube, dresses in another and so on. Then she just slipped the prepacked cubes into the drawers of whatever hotel she checked into. Adah envied her mother's ability to easily and neatly transition from place to place. But Adah had never made any effort to take on those qualities for herself.

Biting the proverbial bullet, she slid the keycard in and opened her door. "Come on in."

Inside was the same disorder she'd left. Clothes all over the bed and the chair near the window. Her suitcase gaped open on the dresser with her other bathing suit and underwear spilling out. She grabbed clothes from the chair and tossed them on top of the suitcase.

"Sit." She scrubbed a hand self-consciously over her windblown hair. "I'm going to have a quick shower—just make yourself comfortable."

"Don't be silly. It's okay, darling."

But Adah hadn't forgotten her mother's earlier comment about her getting cleaned up. "It won't take me long. Sit and play some music on your iPad or something."

Then she seized the nearest item of clothing on the suitcase and rushed to the bathroom. Barely fifteen minutes later, she walked out, running a brush over her hair, her body freshly lotioned and wearing the fitted floral sundress her best friend had insisted she bring to Aruba.

"Inject some sexy in your life, Adah," Selene had told her as she pressed a large department store bag full of dresses and underwear she'd gotten nearly free in her job as a fashion buyer.

Adah felt like a fraud in the garment, effortlessly

pretty in a way she couldn't pull off in her everyday
life. It felt like she was playing dress up, or at least
trying to be like her mother. But she swept those
thoughts away. Refreshed from her rushed shower,
she twisted her straightened hair into a quick top-
knot.

"What brings you here, Mother?"

"My only daughter, of course." Her mother had
truly made herself comfortable, streaming a Luther
Vandross song from the small iPad on her lap. She
shut it down by closing the cover and set it aside. "I
didn't want you to feel all alone in this strange new
place by yourself," she continued.

"I'm not alone, Mother. There are thousands of
tourists on the island this time of year, not to mention all the people who live here."

"You know what I mean. You're always going
someplace by yourself. I think you'd be tired of that
sort of solitary existence by now."

Her mother had grown up in a boisterous home
as one of six children and often voiced regrets she
hadn't had another child after Zoe died.

"With Zoe gone, I'm an only child, Mother. I'm
used to being alone. Most times I prefer it." *Like now.*

"Nonsense." Her mother made a dismissive motion. "Nobody really likes being alone. But I can only
be with you for a little while. There's some business
back home in Atlanta I need to tend to." The business
that had shaped the course of all their lives since it
started. "I came to treat you to something nice for

your birthday. I know your father and I were so busy last month we didn't get a chance to celebrate with you properly."

Weeks before they'd done the annual dinner at Adah's favorite restaurant but hadn't had time for the separate weekend trip to Saint Simons Island that was also part of the birthday tradition.

"It's okay. I know with the company being in trouble, you and Daddy don't have as much time as usual."

"That's no excuse, darling. And that's the reason why I'm here!" Her mother looked excited about whatever she was about to reveal. "I moved you to one of the rooms on the top floor and reserved a half day's pampering session in the most *beautiful* spa. The masseuses there are award winning—although I didn't know massage was something you could get awards for." Her mother frowned like she was giving serious thought to her last remark.

"Mother, you really didn't have to." Adah had come to Aruba by herself to think. The key part of that being *by herself.*

"I know. But I want to." Her mother leaned forward with an even bigger smile. "Our appointments are tomorrow morning. They'll pick us up from here at ten. And while we're gone, they'll move your things up to the new room."

And that was that.

Adah immediately knew her mother's ploy for what it was. And she was half surprised at its transparency. A bribe to get the wedding show on the road and pull the family business out of the fire in which it had found itself despite her parents' brilliance and the relative success of its line of natural hair care products. Still, she allowed it all to happen, the ever-present guilt pricking her into saying yes to whatever it was her mother wanted.

Her twin, Zoe, had died when they were just eleven years old. A car accident on the way home from a young entrepreneurs' summer camp. It was beyond awful that her sister, her best friend, had died. Adah had forced Zoe to sit on the passenger side of the car's back seat just because she'd wanted to sit behind the driver for a reason she couldn't even remember now. The guilt about that still tore her apart. Even at eleven years old, Zoe had been the one eager to take over the family business and make it even better. All Adah had wanted was a job where she could be surrounded by children and hear their laughter all day.

In the end, as co-owner of an exclusive day care complex in North Atlanta catering to some of the city's wealthiest residents, Adah had gotten the job she'd wanted. Zoe had gotten nothing but death.

The next morning, after a restless night spent with her mother on the other side of the wall in an adjoining room, Adah woke and pulled on the same sundress from the afternoon before and the leather sandals. The car that came to get them smelled of the spa, something vaguely citrusy and clean, making her feel as if she were already resting on a masseuse's table and waiting to be transported to boneless relaxation. But she knew peace wouldn't come. Her mother had something to say, and she would state it when she thought Adah was most vulnerable—while she was getting her massage.

She did try to relax during the car ride through the bright and tourist-rich streets of Oranjestad, the car's engine purring through roundabouts and past casinos that burped out victims of the previous night's gambling excesses. Her mother sat across from her, looking content and refreshed, like she'd had the good night's sleep Adah had been denied, her hair perfectly put together in a gray ponytail resting over her shoulder, an ocean-green dress complementing the slender lines of her body.

"You don't really have to do any of this," Adah said.

"I know, darling. But I want to do this for you. It'll mellow you. Besides, after this, your father and I will feel better about not doing enough for your birthday."

Her mother plucked a slice of pineapple from the silver dish sitting between them. Juice exploded from the fruit and dripped down the side of her mouth. On another person, it would have looked clumsy, but her mother's delighted laughter and the delicate way she wiped the juice from her mouth with one of the cloth napkins made her seem charming and young.

Not for the first time, Adah wished she had been the child her mother deserved, a truer reflection of her instead of this awkward and too-soft girl-woman who barely knew how to style herself.

Adah drank from a bottle of water, not wanting to chance any fruit on her dress. With her luck, one of the dark red strawberries would squirt out of her mouth and down her front, making it looked like she'd just suffered a massive nosebleed. Or a mugging.

In the spa, beautiful women in white whisked Adah and her mother away to a serene room that smelled even more like tranquility, this time with low, strings-heavy music and dim lighting. The women gave them fluffy white robes to change into and plied them with cucumber-infused water. An old Deep Forest album, humming with the sounds of chirping birds overlaid by timid violins, played in the background.

Once she was lying on a massage table, with her mother in an identical position a few feet away, Adah actually tried to relax. A silent masseuse began to work on her face, smoothing eucalyptus-scented circles over her forehead and cheeks, while her mother shared stories about what Adah had missed in Atlanta the single day she'd been gone.

"And Petra doesn't seem like the type to fall for someone that shallow, or scary," her mother said, continuing her portion of a conversation Adah was barely paying attention to.

She was talking about a bank manager friend of theirs who'd hooked up with the cold but slightly scandalous anchor of a national news network based in Atlanta. On the outside, Petra seemed boring, and everyone she knew was stuck wondering how she'd managed to snag a man like Gabriel Saint.

"Every woman has something about them that only appeals to a select few people," Adah said. Petra kept things pretty low-key and had a wicked sense of humor she often kept hidden. "Petra is a badass," Adah said. "She just doesn't show that side of herself very often."

"Well, one person must have seen it, and I mean Gabriel Saint, because everyone is mystified about them being together."

"Including you?"

"Including me."

Adah smiled as much as the hands moving on her face would allow. "You only see what you want to see."

Her mother laughed, not admitting to the truth they both knew. And it was so comfortable talking with her about the old familiar things that Adah *did* actually relax.

But then her mother said, "Have you been giving much thought to the wedding, darling?"

Adah released a slow breath through her nose. "No, I haven't." The masseuse paused with her hands on the suddenly tense muscles of Adah's thigh. After a quick glance at Adah's face, she continued the massage.

"You know Errol and Stephanie are excited to officially welcome you into their family." Errol and Stephanie Randal were onetime rivals and now potential in-laws of Adah's, owners of Leilani's Pearls, a successful bath-and-beauty business that was on the verge of the same kind of stagnation pulling down Palmer-Mitchell Naturals. Separately the two companies would flounder, but by joining together they stood a greater chance of succeeding in the increasingly competitive marketplace.

Just about every beauty company had some kind of natural-hair product line now, even companies who'd created their success from selling perms to black women. Despite being in business for over thirty years, Palmer-Mitchell Naturals was a relatively new company and not well-known enough to succeed on its own.

Palmer-Mitchell Naturals needed Leilani's Pearls much more than the other way around. And the agreement to merge companies, and do it in a way that kept the businesses in the family, hinged on Adah's agreement to marry the Randal's son, Bennett. The idea for Adah to become the sacrificial wife had come from her mother during a time of romantic disappointment and on the anniversary of her sister's death. Marinating in pain from all sides, Adah could think only that the less useful sister had survived.

"I know the Randals are anxious, Mother. I know you and Daddy are, too." Her stomach clenched with unease, and she wished she could just say yes and agree to the date without putting her parents through all this worry. Any relaxation she'd gained from the massage had fled. Her muscles felt tight and unwieldy.

"I want you to be certain about your decision, Adah. When I first suggested this idea, you were a young woman in college, practically still a child. I know you're a different person now."

But the situation Palmer-Mitchell Naturals found itself in was the same. Adah pressed her lips together while the anxiety rolled through her, steady and unrelenting. The masseuse's fingers dug harder into her back.

"But—" her mother's tone changed "—think about how amazing this would be for you, too. You could have the financial freedom to realize your dreams. And have a handsome husband to call your own."

As if all Adah had ever wanted from this thing was a man.

She twitched under a particularly firm press of the masseuse's fingers. "I know I agreed to all this before, but I just need a little time right now."

Her mother sighed. "I know, darling. I know."

Then she noticeably withdrew into herself, leaving the room silent except for the sounds of the women's hands on their skin, oil rubbing into flesh and quiet breathing. Embarrassment at airing their dirty laundry in such a relatively public place heated

Adah's face. Although it hadn't been a full-fledged fight, she felt battered and in the wrong. Her mother had always come away from their arguments as the clear victor while Adah was left limping and bleeding in her separate corner. This time was no different. She sighed into the deafening silence.

Later, Adah tried to recapture some of the light-hearted conversation they'd been having before. But her heart wasn't in it, and it was obvious. Soon enough, their spa day was finished. Adah's body was limp from the massage, but her mind was wound too tightly to rest.

After the car dropped them off at the hotel, Adah and her mother picked up the keys to their new rooms and took the elevator up. The penthouse room was beautiful. But Adah gave it no more than a passing glance before she grabbed her jogging clothes and quickly changed.

"I'm going out," she called out through the open door between their rooms, then left before her mother could reply.

Adah took the stairs. Her sneakered feet pounded on the elegant steps, taking her down five flights, away from her mother and the snaking guilt that wouldn't let her say no outright to the gift of an upgrade. For so much of her twenty-six years, Adah felt she'd been stealing her life. A charmed existence taken away from her sister, who'd died before she'd even fully known what she had. Parents who loved her. Parents who could afford to send her to private school. Who had the strength and brilliance to start a small business that became a national company within Adah's lifetime. Her parents wanted more. Adah wanted more. But she knew the things they wanted were no longer compatible with her own wants, if they ever were.

At the bottom floor, she panted rough and ragged, sweat covering her body, heat flowing through her like she wished some new strength would. She was tired of this weakness of hers in the face of her parents' wishes. Marriage was a serious thing. If she couldn't find a man of her own, she'd rather be alone than with someone she wasn't in love with.

The messed-up thing was that she actually liked Bennett Randal. They'd known each other for years and were like brother and sister. But he wasn't someone she wanted to marry. At first, she thought she would be able to do it, but the idea of being with him in *that* way had unsettled her more and more as the years passed. Bennett, she knew, didn't have the qualms she did.

He expected the marriage to happen. While the details were being finalized, he was enjoying being a bachelor, gobbling up all the available sex he could, usually via the hottest reality stars in Atlanta and the world, before he was tied to Adah forever.

Forever.

Just the thought of it made her breath stutter. And

it wasn't just because she was running full speed out of the hotel and onto the beach. Her feet pushed into the soft sand, and she forced herself to take even breaths, trying to put as much distance from her troubles as possible while not getting one step ahead of them.

Adah squeezed her eyes tightly for a moment but kept pace along the beach, which was nearly empty; most of the beachgoers had gone inside for showers and dinner and sex. The moon was fat and gorgeous in the Aruban sky. A paradise. Or it would be if her mother and Adah's own troubles hadn't followed her here.

She ran on. Her breath huffing. The sound of her feet thumping against the sand and the waves rushing up toward her but never touching. A writhing shape in the water pulled her attention from her breath's steady rhythm. The moon glided over whatever it was, showing hints of curves. A couple, she thought, making love in the water and under the stars. She changed her path and ran in an arc away from the water, giving whoever it was their privacy.

But as she moved away, the splashing grew more intense and moved closer to the beach; then a lone body climbed from the water. Adah's footsteps slowed as details of the swimmer emerged under the moonlight. A masculine body firm with muscles apparent even in the dark, bare shoulders, torso and hips. She stared, her footsteps slowing. Was this man naked?

"Doe Eyes?"

She stumbled at the familiar voice and nickname, then without fully realizing it, began walking toward the water's edge and the gorgeous creature emerging from the water, getting barer as the moonlight slid silver fingers over every hard inch of him.

"Ah," Kingsley said, his breath coming quickly after his swim. "I figured I would see you again."

Adah clenched her jaw to stop her tongue from hanging out of her mouth. Kingsley wasn't naked, but he might as well have been. The moonlight outlined him from the top of his proud head to his feet striding out of the water and across the sand to meet her. Pale swim trunks clung to his hips, to the insistent shape between his legs, and the tops of his muscled thighs that were wide and hard enough to make the tips of her fingers ache to sink into them.

He just said something. It's my turn to talk now. She swallowed again.

"I'm just going for a jog to escape my troubles," Adah finally said with her wryest smile. She looked down the beach and saw the illuminated outline of her hotel much farther away than she'd realized.

Damn. How far had she come?

"Should we call it destiny then?" Kingsley wiped the seawater from his face, dragging his hand from his chin down to his strong throat and chiseled chest. Even in the soft light and pervasive dark, Adah could see his grin.

"Let's just call it a coincidence and leave it at that," she said, crossing her arms over nipples that had gone embarrassingly tight.

Kingsley stepped even closer, and she resisted the urge to close the last few feet of space between them and see if his body was as hard or smooth as it looked.

She cleared her throat. "Aren't you afraid they'll cart you off for public indecency?"

He looked down at himself and shrugged. "They'd be false charges if they do," he said, grinning. "Do you think I'm being indecent just by swimming at night? I have a suit on."

"What you call a bathing suit some might call underwear." And the fact that it was a pair of tight white trunks only highlighted what a dark bathing suit would hide. Not that he had anything to be ashamed about. Heat scalded her cheeks, and she yanked her gaze up from his crotch.

"I'm more covered than most people on the beach today," Kingsley said.

He was right. On her walk, she'd seen dozens of European tourists spread across the beach, all body types and speaking so many languages that she'd lost track of how many she heard. But the one thing most had in common was that nearly all the men wore brief swim shorts that clung to their butts and crotches, being just as aggressively sexy as the women in their bikinis. Adah was all for equal opportunity swimwear and enjoyed her walks mostly because of the view. Not all the men were beautiful, but the ones who were gave her quite the eyeful.

She'd been impressed and amused until she saw the more modestly covered Kingsley on the kite and just about lost her mind. Not that she was doing that great of a job of managing herself now. And if his smug grin was anything to go by, he saw through her clearly enough.

Adah could only laugh at herself. "Anyway, it was great to see you, *all* of you." She couldn't resist. "But I've got to get going."

"Nope." Kingsley shook his head. "You can't leave yet."

"Excuse me?"

"I want to see you again, and I don't want fate to determine the time and place."

She should say no. Adah shook her head and pressed her lips together, just on the edge of the confession. "You know I can't…" But she didn't know how to finish that sentence.

"This is nothing more than an invitation to go snorkeling," Kingsley said with a look that was far from innocent. "Aruba has some of the most beautiful waters in the Caribbean. You should experience it with locals who know what they're doing."

"And you're one of these locals?"

"Not at all, but my friends are and they will be there. I'm only local to Miami." He said his home city with an echo of pride in his voice.

Miami was so very far from Atlanta. *Good.* That meant nothing could come of this…whatever it was. No matter how much Adah's eyes drifted low on his body and her heart sped up at the thought of him touching her. But it wasn't all because he was the most perfect male specimen she'd ever seen. He was just so open with his desire for her, so deliriously transparent in a way she'd never experienced before that it was intoxicating. And she also felt like the very air around him smelled of freedom. Escape. A higher plane of living, where pleasure was easy and everything else was inconsequential.

"What exactly do you have in mind?" she asked.

His beautiful teeth flashed in the moonlight again, and her breathing sped up. This was beyond ridiculous.

"We have a snorkeling trip planned for tomorrow night."

She gestured to the high moon and the inky evening around them. "Snorkeling at night? Doesn't that defeat the purpose?"

"Not at all. The sea looks completely different at night, just beautiful. You won't regret it."

Adah started to argue with herself about the safety of going off someplace with a man she didn't know. But all her life she'd been safe.

"Okay." She took a deep breath once she'd committed herself. "Where should I meet you?"

"Do you know where the lighthouse is?"

"Yes." It rose high and majestic, a historic piece

of island history where tourists gathered from morning until night to take pictures, gawk at the scenery and buy food and drinks from the vendors who set up shop at its base.

"Meet me there just before sunset," Kingsley said.

She raised an eyebrow at him. The snorkeling trip now sounded suspiciously like a date. It lay at the back of her tongue to change her mind and tell him there was something else she'd committed to after all. But she bit back the almost-confession.

"Okay," Adah said. "I'll meet you there. Near sunset."

"Perfect."

Adah didn't know about that. She was quite possibly doing the most *imperfect* thing for her situation right now. She didn't need another man in the mix to cloud her already-murky judgment where the potential wedding was concerned. But as she turned away to jog back down the beach toward her hotel and her mother, her mind's eye wouldn't let go of the memory of Kingsley, rising from the water like some Adonis thirst trap, making her heart beat fast and her tongue feel heavy in her mouth, thick with the desire to taste the path where every drop of water had run.

Yeah. Her decision making was cloudy. Absolutely the cloudiest it had been in a long time. But that didn't stop her from smiling the whole way back to the hotel.

Seconds after walking into her room, she heard a knock on the other side of the door joining her room to her mother's, then a muffled voice. Instead of answering what was undoubtedly the question of where she'd just come from, she quickly fled to the bathroom, stripped and turned on the shower. Her mother's questions would have to wait another day.

Chapter 3

Kingsley watched Doe Eyes run down the beach
and away from him. He still didn't know her name,
and that stirred something illicit in him he never
knew existed. She wasn't beautiful in the way he'd
grown used to seeing in Miami. She was all klutzy
librarian charm with her subtle curves and hidden
smiles. And she was *interested*. He'd have to be blind
and deaf not to notice the way she responded to him,
feminine and helpless, stirring both his lust and the
urge to protect her.

Even from across the sand, he had heard her
breath catch when she saw him. And he'd felt every
second of her long stare at his body, her eyes drift-
ing across his shoulders, his chest and lower while

they talked. It was a change from how things were at home when he was Kingsley Diallo, CEO of Diallo Corporation and dressed in his bespoke suits, backed by his family's billions of dollars.

Damn, Doe Eyes was gorgeous.

The way she wanted him made him desire her even more. She watched him with a hunger he felt to the very tip of his toes. His sex had twitched with more than a little interest the longer she stared with the lust so naked on her face. It had been a true miracle he hadn't popped out of his swim trunks and announced to her in no uncertain terms just how very interested he was.

Kingsley drew a deep breath and walked the rest of the way up the beach.

"Should I give you a second to get yourself together?" A voice came from behind the red glow of a cigarette.

His friend Gage sat high up on the sand, almost invisible except for his cigarette and the faint trails of smoke that the wind blew behind him. When the clouds parted, he got a brief view of Gage's curly hair pulled to the top of his head in a man bun, his bare chest and the tattered jean shorts that sagged around his narrow hips.

"Don't be an ass." But Kingsley *did* need a moment to get his head back in the game. Doe Eyes drew him like the sweetest honey, but she was also hiding something. A secret she didn't want him to know. He saw it in the shift of her dark eyes.

He dropped down onto the blanket beside Gage and watched the path Doe Eyes had taken away from him.

"I invited her to the snorkeling trip tomorrow night."

"I heard." Gage ashed his cigarette in the sand beside him. "Do you think that's wise?"

"It's not like I invited her to an orgy or something equally inappropriate."

"Is there such a thing as an orgy of one?" The glowing end of the cigarette made a figure eight in the air as Gage gestured.

"Even I'm not that good." Kingsley grunted.

"After you're done with her, that girl will probably disagree." His friend laughed, a flash of white teeth in the dark. "I've heard the rumors." Kingsley wasn't exactly celibate, not in Miami or here in Aruba.

"Why do you always think I'm out to get some?"

"Aren't you? It's dark as hell out here, but I can still see that woman is stunning and that she's smitten with you. Good odds are you'll have her in your bed in zero minutes flat. Just be prepared for the consequences."

But that was the thing about being away from his responsibilities for the summer. He didn't worry about potential problems. He didn't pay attention to projections and outlooks. He smelled the roses, plucked them if he felt like it, then left them scattered in his wake in mutually satisfying, casual encounters. Enjoyment was something he very much believed in during the normal course of his life. While in Aruba for the summer, it was the very air he breathed.

He almost reached for Gage's clove cigarette to take a drag, both because it smelled so good and to illustrate a point in that one carefree motion. All this was casual. There would be no issues. Doe Eyes was a woman with secrets and a woman, whether or not she was aware of it, in search of passion. He would enjoy plucking the secret from between her lips, from between her thighs. But more than that, he would enjoy bringing and sharing pleasure with her, sweet and deep as the sea around Aruba. Free of commitment and full of all the joy two people could know together.

"Consequences don't belong in a place like this," he settled for saying.

Gage laughed again, the hand holding his cigarette balanced on one upraised knee. The sound of his mirth was loud on the nearly deserted beach.

Kingsley did reach for the cigarette then, plucked it from his friend's hand, and took a deep and slow drag. Sweet smoke filled his throat with a delicious burn before he blew it out into the night. He squinted against the smoke, and the wind carried the gray tendrils toward the steadily disappearing shape of Doe Eyes jogging away from him and toward wherever it was that she'd come from.

"I'm just having a little fun," he said.

Gage took his cigarette back and waved it toward

the woman Kingsley couldn't get out of his mind. "Be careful that fun doesn't come back to bite you in the ass, and not in a good way."

When Kingsley got back to his house—bought nearly six years ago now—from hanging out with Gage, a message about work was waiting for him. Never mind that it was nearly three o'clock in the morning.

"I think we should diversify," his mother said on his voice mail.

This was something she'd been saying for a while. Diallo Corporation had built one of the strongest names in beauty and skin care, but his mother—and chief operations officer—thought that they, like Facebook, had to constantly innovate in order to stay relevant and profitable. He'd just about fallen out of his chair when she'd mentioned Facebook, but he kept an open mind. She wanted them to take on something else, maybe hair care, she wasn't quite sure, but something that would keep Diallo Corporation profitable, visible and on the list of the Fortune 500.

His mother wanted this, but it was up to Kingsley to find out what that next thing was. He already had an idea but wanted to discuss it with her when he was back at home and behind his imported mahogany desk, not when he was about to be naked in his small house more than a thousand miles away from the nearest Diallo.

He sent her a quick email in response.

I agree. Will talk more about this when I get back in two weeks. In the meantime, relay all communications regarding this matter to Carter.

His brother, Carter, didn't have an official title at the company, but he was jokingly called the Magic Man. Along with Kingsley, he knew how to transform nearly any idea related to Diallo Corporation into something viable.

After sending the email, Kingsley groaned and rolled the beginnings of tension out of his neck. He'd only been on the island a day and a half, barely a fourth of the time he usually spent away from his family responsibilities. He wasn't going to let business get in the way of his time off. He pulled off his swim trunks and tossed them in the laundry basket on his way to the shower.

A long time ago, he'd learned to be strict with his vacation time. If he wasn't, no one else would be. His family could talk to him at any time about personal matters, but he was strict about company affairs. Not now. Never here.

Kingsley allowed the steaming water to wash away the remnants of his irritation about his mother's voice mail. He soaped his body from head to toe with body wash, easing the seawater from his skin, then used the washcloth to scrub himself until his skin stung and all he could smell was the mandarin orange scent. He rubbed himself down to pure sensation, the water on his skin, the heat sinking into his muscles, the anticipation of how good Doe Eyes would feel under him.

Truly, he had no intention of seducing her on the snorkeling trip. But his body didn't believe what his mind was saying. He hardened at the thought of her, an inexorable arousal that left him winded.

He pressed his palm against the tile while steam rose around him, water running down the muscles of his back, his butt and his thighs. No, he had no intention of making a move on her. But he wanted. Oh, he *wanted*. And it was with that want sizzling through his veins that he allowed the greed for her to move his hand low and squeeze the breath from his lungs until he was painting the tiles with the hot spurt of his satisfaction. Breathless from the water that still ran over him, the release only made him want the real thing even more.

Kingsley hissed as he touched his sensitive flesh and imagined her mouth. Her body. Her everything.

He groaned and dropped his forehead against the tile, not even the least bit satisfied by his self-delivered orgasm.

Tomorrow, the devil at the back of his mind said. *Tomorrow you can have her.* Kingsley groaned again, and the sound echoed back to him, torture and pleasure, in the enclosed room.

The next evening, he wasn't sure she would come. Yes, he had invited her. Yes, she wanted him.

But there was no certainty. So when he got to the lighthouse, the other three people set to go on the snorkeling trip already waiting down by the beach and having their own pre-sunset party, he only half-expected to see Doe Eyes.

But she was there, wearing a one-piece swimsuit, jean shorts and a short-sleeved shirt partially unbuttoned over it all. His breath stopped at the sight of her, then started again. She stood at the base of the lighthouse, talking to one of the vendors selling coconut water and smoothies. The straps of a backpack hung from one of her shoulders.

She was early by nearly half an hour, the sun barely beginning to fall toward the horizon. The bright sunlight haloed her with the bowl of the green coconut in her hand, as she took occasional sips from the straw sticking up from the coconut. The vendor, old enough to be her father and missing several teeth, laughed when she said something, and she made a face before joining in his laughter.

Damn. She was so gorgeous. Body sleek and compelling in the shorts that barely contained the splendor of her behind. It was hot, much warmer than even the previous days, and the winds weren't nearly as strong. Sweat lined her forehead, the soft skin of her throat. From where he stood, Kingsley could even make out the swell of her breasts under the loose, short-sleeved shirt and bathing suit.

Okay, now he was being creepy.

He cleared his throat and took a single step toward

her, still keeping a respectful distance. He couldn't remember the last time he was so ridiculously horny over a woman, a near stranger at that. He shoved his hands in his pockets, as much to appear casual as to hide the beginnings of interest his body already showed.

"Doe Eyes."

She looked over her shoulder at him, still laughing, then turned back to the man to say her goodbyes before sauntering over to Kingsley with the coconut in her hand.

"Don't you think it's a little ridiculous to keep calling me that?" But she didn't look offended in the least. Instead she looked amused, smiling again in a way that teased, not open and friendly but with a corner of her mouth pressed between her teeth as if she was keeping part of her amusement to herself.

"Until I know your name, I think that suits you just fine."

She shook her head and opened her mouth like she was about to say something, maybe even her name, but something over his shoulder must have caught her eye because she gasped. Kingsley turned. All he could see was the restaurant, the view of the water and the sky turning to a fiery amber.

"This place is beautiful…" she said with breathless wonder.

Her face glowed with the excitement of what she saw, her eyes widening and the curve of her mouth unfurling to shape a real and complete smile for the first time since he'd met her.

"It is very nice."

"I…I guess I just haven't been paying attention." Her eyes were still focused on the lowering sun and the colors streaming across the sky. "I've had a lot on my mind," she said in a low and faraway voice.

By the look on her face, all those things that had occupied her thoughts just got burned away by the flaming splendor of the sky. She was gorgeous. And watching her, Kingsley wondered if at any point during his many trips to Aruba whether he'd ever taken the time to appreciate the beauty of the island like this. But the setting sun was nothing compared to the woman with her wide doe eyes, drinking up all the colors flaring overhead.

The others going on the trip—Carlos, Steven and Annika—were down on the beach, sipping their beers and talking around a small fire they'd made in the sand. Their boat was anchored in the small cove nearby and sheltered from the rocks. They were waiting for Kingsley to return with the woman he'd told them about. But he could afford to let Doe Eyes appreciate the sunset for a few more minutes.

"We can go closer," he said.

She murmured something that might have been her assent, and he guided her carefully toward the overlook with a plaque detailing the history of the lighthouse and the ship that had smashed itself to pieces on the rocks more than a hundred years before on its way somewhere else.

Doe Eyes leaned against the railing, watching the sky and occasionally blindly seeking the straw in the coconut with her mouth. For the first time since he'd seen her watching him, she was completely unguarded. It suited her.

He smiled at the way she seemed to unconsciously lean into his shoulder with her eyes trained on the horizon, watching the slow fall of the sun into the sea. The flash of light grew increasingly dim until the sun fell completely in the water and the sky glowed with the remnants of its flame.

"I could see this every day," she breathed.

"We have similar sunsets in Miami," he said although he didn't know where that came from.

"Similar but not the same."

"Similar but not the same," he agreed.

Miami was unquestionably striking to him. Just the way that Jamaica, the island where his grandparents were born and where his immediate family returned year after year, was the most beautiful place in the world to him. And he'd been around the world enough to see most of the competition.

"You should see Jamaica if you haven't already," he told her, pressing his shoulder into hers. "The sunsets there will make you cry."

She laughed and turned briefly to him, the sunset's colors brushing her face in shades of amber. "Have they made you cry?"

"Not yet, but I'm a hard sell."

She laughed again; this time he could see the distance in the smile that lingered, that her attention was no longer on the sky and the joy it made her feel.

"You ready to get going?" he asked.

She bit the corner of her lip. "Yes."

He waited for her to finish the coconut; then took her down to the beach where the others waited. She walked just ahead of him, watching his three friends sitting around the fire with a mixture of wariness and relief, obviously having suspected that it would just be the two of them after all.

"We didn't think you'd make it back," Carlos said in Spanish. With his cropped hair, thick beard and full-sleeve tattoos, he looked like a typical hipster.

"I can see why," Annika said in Dutch, smiling widely at Doe Eyes. "She's pretty. How did you manage to find such a hot woman to play with after being on the island only a few days?"

Steven, serious and slender in his designer T-shirt and matching shorts, watched all the action like someone at a tennis match, gaze moving back and forth between the players.

Kingsley shook his head. "English, guys." Then he laughingly introduced her as Doe Eyes, enduring his friends' inevitable teasing that the woman he wanted hadn't even told him her name.

"I speak a decent amount of Spanish," Doe Eyes said. "If it makes you feel more comfortable speaking your own languages, it's okay with me."

Annika laughed. "We love her!" she crowed in English, then jumped up from her cross-legged seat near the fire to hug Doe Eyes, who grinned widely and hugged Annika tightly in return.

"Hi!"

"I might just love her, too," Carlos said, this time in Dutch, as he watched the two women, dark and light, as they hugged.

"Pervert," Kingsley muttered.

"Not at all, just a lover of women."

Steven greeted her in his subdued way, squeezing her hand before sinking back down into a graceful lotus on the sand. He wrestled a beer from the depths of the cooler and gave it to Doe Eyes.

"Thanks for being okay with me coming out with you all," she said, looking at each face around the fire. "I've never gone snorkeling at night, but Kingsley says it's safe." The lilt in her voice plainly asked them to confirm the safety of what she was about to do.

"It *is* safe," Steven confirmed. "I've done it more times than I can count."

Annika nodded. "It'll be fun. Even though I've lived in Aruba for nearly two years, I haven't done it before. But Kingsley said it's something I absolutely have to try."

"He's very convincing," Carlos said. "I swear if he said I had to eat fire to be a real Aruban, I would do it even though he doesn't know a damn thing about being from here."

"Or about fire," Kingsley said with a laugh.

"It burns," Doe Eyes murmured, looking at him.

Kingsley locked eyes with her. "It certainly does."

Annika laughed, her pale blue eyes brimming with mirth. It was embarrassingly obvious she knew what Kingsley was up to. Yes, if he got the chance he would absolutely sleep with Doe Eyes. Well, not exactly sleep. He wanted to make long and deep love with her, press her into any available surface and show her just how much he knew about making a woman feel good. Kingsley cleared his throat and sat on the side of the fire opposite her, hiding the sudden tightness at his crotch with his beer.

They finished their drinks while the lights in the sky faded into gray, leaving trails of dark against the paleness of the moon. Dusk amplified the light from the crackling fire, a signal for them to get ready.

Steven was the first one to stand up. "Ready whenever you guys are."

Although Steven had been the one to organize the trip, he'd asked Kingsley to give the prep talk to the group about the particulars of night snorkeling and partnering up. He also passed out the waterproof flashlights. Annika snickered when Kingsley announced he was partnering with Doe Eyes even after he told her the obvious reason, which was that Doe Eyes hadn't done a night dive before and would need all the help she could get.

"But what about me?" Annika asked with a mischievous grin, determined to torture him. "I'm a newbie, too."

At a look from Kingsley, Steven grabbed her by the waist and pulled her off toward the boat anchored nearby.

With everyone else sitting in the small motorboat, Kingsley pushed it into the water. Once it was far enough, he released the anchor and climbed in. Steven started the engine and it growled, propelling them toward the place where the sun had disappeared nearly half an hour before. The engine's noise took away the silence, and the five of them were lost in their own thoughts and in the beauty of the night as they raced toward the reefs.

Kingsley sat across from Doe Eyes, watching the beach and their banked fire get smaller and smaller. Nervousness vibrated from her, and he wanted very much to slide closer to her and convince her nothing would happen tonight she didn't want to. The sea was a vast and frightening place. But that didn't mean he would allow her to disappear beneath it.

"Here we are," Steven said. He cut the engine.

In the sudden silence, the boat bobbed in the dark water, the sound of the sea slapping gently against the hull.

"Here" was far away from shore and nowhere in sight of their fire at all. There was nothing but the dark and writhing water around them.

"It's a little creepy out here," Annika muttered, most of her bravado gone.

"Yeah, but it's nice," Carlos said. "The quiet is very soothing."

Doe Eyes sat with her hands curled around the edge of the boat, the fear slowly clearing from her face the longer they sat in the quiet with the sound of the water lapping at the boat.

Kingsley leaned close to her. "You okay?"

She jumped, looking away from the dark and rippling water. "Yeah. I'm fine. This is just…it's all new to me. Amazing. Scary."

He lifted his gaze from her to take in their surroundings, trying to pretend the others weren't watching every move they made. "Facing the things that scare you is a great way to grow."

Doe Eyes snorted. "And to get eaten by a shark, too, I'm sure."

"No shark bites here." Kingsley pulled off his shirt to show his unscarred belly in the moonlight. Annika snickered, having apparently gotten over her own nervousness. He thought he saw a smile from Doe Eyes. When her hands loosened from the edge of the boat, he considered his mission of distraction a success. He shoved his shirt in his waterproof pack while Annika laughed at him outright.

"Gear up, everyone," Steven said, unsuccessfully hiding his own laughter.

Although there had been a quick tutorial on the beach, Kingsley stayed close to Doe Eyes to make sure she put on her gear properly. Despite her obvious nervousness, she put on her snorkel and fins with easy and practiced movements, checking the fit and the security and brightness of the flashlight secured to her wrists, while everyone else did the same. After a quick verbal check all around, the group slipped into the water. Kingsley and Doe Eyes were the last.

"Ready?"

"Absolutely." She looked like she was trying to convince herself, and he wondered why. But he mentally shrugged and slipped into the water first, keeping his head above the surface and his body close to the anchored boat. He flicked on his flashlight. In his board shorts and otherwise bare skin, he felt the pressure of the water, the night's brisk breeze on his face and neck. A shiver of reaction climbed up his spine.

She sat in the belly of the boat for a moment, watching him, then walked to the very edge, took a quick breath and splashed down beside him. The splatter of water made her blink her eyes behind the mask, and he floated away from the boat slowly, signaling for her to follow him.

His flashlight illuminated a long line of water around them, pushing aside the shadows and, he hoped, any potential fear for her. She brushed against him briefly, and he felt her tremble. Then she adjusted her mask, gave him the thumbs-up, turned her face into the water and began to explore. After a moment Kingsley began to do the same.

The reef was close to the surface. Only a few feet separated the tips of Kingsley's fins from the coral alive with color and darting fish whose scales shimmered under the light from their torches. Sea urchins, spiny and dangerous, poked out from holes in the coral. Kingsley tapped her shoulder and pointed to make sure she saw them.

This wasn't Kingsley's first time snorkeling at night. He'd even done some night diving, traveling down to the ocean floor to watch octopi, their bodies dotted with phosphorescence, slide along the coral. He'd swum through massive schools of brilliantly colored fish not present during the day. All of it had been breathtaking.

But there was nothing like the wonder on this woman's face, her eyes widening, hands clutching fiercely at his when she saw something new: the powerful and steadily moving sea through the beams of their torches, large schools of bright blue parrot fish swimming lazily in the night waters. He wanted to show her more. He wanted her to see everything.

This feeling wasn't a new one, wanting to preen and introduce a woman to the best of what he knew. What was new to him was the lack of urgency. Kingsley enjoyed the brush of her arm against his, rising up to the surface to take a breath and catch sight of the twin globes of her bottom resting on top of the water. It was a deep and pure pleasure he could bask in for hours. But despite the vague possibility of this unnamed and beautiful woman disappearing from his life at any moment, he wasn't frantic in his desire for her.

He knew he would have her.

Still, his ache to touch her was almost a painful thing, a desire that clung to the backs of his teeth and burned steadily. It was slow. It was hot. And it easily melted away the memory of any other woman he'd ever wanted.

In just his mask and fins, he swam farther down, holding his breath and lighting up the darkness for her. Deeper into the water, he saw a school of spotted turquoise fish, their scales bright even in the small grotto where they hid. Kingsley propelled himself up to the surface, taking a deep breath when he hit fresh air. She took out her snorkel.

"You okay?"

He nodded yes. "There's something you should see, lower."

Her eyes widened. "This is snorkeling, not diving," she said.

"You can handle it."

She gave him a curious look, then put her mask back on, refitted her snorkel and nodded at him in acceptance of his challenge. Kingsley grinned, took her hand and dove deep with her fingers wrapped tightly around his.

Nearly an hour later, they surfaced for the last time to the sound of MC Solaar playing from the speaker Carlos had brought. It was a miracle they'd gotten any reception on the battered, old thing. Kingsley could hear Annika "singing" along to the old-school French rap and laughing at herself when she tripped over the words. A look at his watch told Kingsley they'd already been out there for nearly three hours and at almost ten o'clock at night, the others were ready to wash off the salt, get someplace dry and drink something a little harder than beer to close out the night.

A sleek head appeared from beneath the surface barely a foot away, and Kingsley smiled at her automatically, having quickly grown used to the brightness of her eyes behind the mask and the way she grinned around the snorkel in excitement at the things they'd found together. He pulled off his mask, and, after a glance around them, she did the same. She wiped water from her face.

"Time to go in, huh?"

"Yup. They've probably been waiting for us a little while."

Doe Eyes didn't hide her disappointed look, but she nodded, cast one look at the glare of his flashlight that illuminated their bodies just under the water. "Let's go then."

Kingsley gestured for her to go first. Once she'd swum a fair distance in front of him, he followed at a leisurely pace, enjoying the last of their privacy.

"I thought you two were going to stay out there until sunrise," Carlos said, blowing a stream of cigarette smoke over his shoulder.

"I'd prune up too much by then," Doe Eyes said. "I value the softness of my skin too much."

"Even at the risk of denying yourself the company of this hunka burnin' love?" Annika tossed a look at Kingsley as he clambered into the boat.

He ignored her and turned up his nose at Carlos.

"The only thing burning up out here is our nose hairs from that cigarette. You couldn't wait until we got back to land to light up, Carlos?" His friend smoked the cheapest and most offensive cigarettes known to humankind, having exchanged his addiction to hard drugs for one to nicotine.

"You know I have a vice, man." Carlos blew another stream of smoke, this time through his clenched teeth.

"Those things will kill you just like the other crap you gave up," Kingsley said. He sensed Doe Eyes watching him with curiosity.

"Not this again." Steven groaned over the long-standing source of disagreement. "Everybody ready?"

After he got the appropriate number of grunts and yeses, he started the boat's engine and propelled them back toward land.

At the beach, Steven anchored the boat and cut the engine. The others moved slowly to get their few belongings, sealed in watertight bags, and climbed from the boat to the beach, where the battery-operated lantern they'd left stuck in the sand still blazed but the fire had long since died. Kingsley felt pleasantly exhausted but didn't want to go back to his place yet. Although his body was tired from the swim, he felt mentally energized by the snorkeling, and by the presence of the woman he couldn't get off his mind.

"I'm tired, but I'm not tired," Carlos said as he zipped up his backpack with the last of his stuff and hefted it onto his back. "You get me?"

"Yeah." Steven sighed with his own exhaustion.

"You don't have to go home," Annika said. "I told you to come over to Elina's place. She's having a thing tonight."

"I'm not going to bust into a party I wasn't invited to," Steven said.

"Consider yourself invited then, damn." Annika rolled her eyes. She was sleeping with Elina and Elina's boyfriend, Alexander.

She dragged her own pack to the sand as she helped Kingsley disassemble their camp on the beach, put away the lamp and the rest of their gear in the anchored boat and under a secured tarp.

"That's good enough for me." Carlos grinned.

"Sounds good." Kingsley didn't give it a second thought. It was either that or invite Doe Eyes back to his place in a shameless attempt at getting into her pants. "You should come," he tossed to her over one shoulder.

Doe Eyes already had her dry clothes back on and, with her backpack on one shoulder, looked ready to head back to her hotel.

"I don't think I can stay out any later than this," she said, regret and reluctance coloring her voice.

Kingsley jumped out of the boat and shouldered his pack. "What, do you have a curfew or something?"

Her shoulders went stiff like someone had just poked her with a pointed stick.

"No, I don't have a *curfew*. You ever thought I might have to get up early tomorrow for something?"

"No. You're here on vacation. Unless you're getting up early for a sunrise wedding or one of those boring-ass island tours they sell to tourists."

She winced again, and Kingsley could feel the others watching them even though half had already climbed into Annika's van. Annika was at the wheel and tossing them occasional annoyed glances. She was ready to go.

"The party should be pretty low-key. Nothing at all to challenge your virtue or your tolerance for loud music," Kingsley said. "But if you get bored or scared, I'll take you home."

His house was only a ten-minute walk from Elina's. If Doe Eyes truly wanted to go home, he could easily take her in his truck. "A win-win situation, really," Kingsley finished.

She looked skeptical but interested, her hips inclined toward him even as she plucked at the frayed edge of her shorts, apparently thinking seriously about the offer of a decent party with good booze and people. "Why does it feel like I'm being lured into the lion's den?"

Kingsley gave her a mock roar. Incredibly, she laughed at his weak joke. "Okay. I'll come."

As soon as she got in the van, Annika drove off, barely giving Kingsley time to pull the door shut.

"Whoa, girl!" He fumbled fast for his seat belt.

"I heard Alexander got that magic tongue," Carlos teased from well out of Annika's reach. "After the bedroom looks you and her—" he jerked his chin at Kingsley and Doe Eyes "—have been giving each other all night, she's eager to get in some lovin' of her own."

"Don't be jealous, Carlos." Annika flashed him a dangerous look. "I told you I can share Alexander with you whenever you're ready."

Steven's shout of laughter drowned out Carlos's response.

With their teasing and laughter, the ride toward the south part of the island passed quickly. They talked about Annika's interesting relationship with the couple, Elina and Alexander, that had lasted well over a year now and was, in her words, more satisfying than any she'd ever had before.

"Doesn't anyone get jealous?" Carlos asked, looking voyeuristically fascinated.

"There's nothing to be jealous of," Annika said with a shrug.

They pulled into the drive of the small house. It had the soft, pulsing beat of trance music pouring from beneath the front door. After a quick rap on the red painted door, Annika pushed it open. Once inside the smell of marijuana smoke and the sound of "Glory Box" greeted them, promising a laid-back, if slightly illegal, vibe. Walking behind Annika, Kingsley stayed just behind Doe Eyes as they made their way into the open living room, whose intimate darkness was amplified by multicolored Christmas lights. It reminded Kingsley of an off-campus college party. He suspected there was a keg or two stashed someplace.

Despite his desire for the opposite, he was ready for Doe Eyes to change her mind and tell him she wanted to go home. Her eyes darted to each face in the room as if trying to make the decision about whether or not to stay based on the expressions she found there.

Everybody seemed like they were having a good time. Some swayed in the center of the living room to the beat of the music with bass heavy enough to vibrate in Kingsley's chest. Others sat in chairs or on the floor, talking or laughing or drinking from their red plastic cups. The house was so full that guests overflowed into the backyard.

"I need a shower," Carlos said from behind Kingsley.

"Go have a shower then," Annika said. "The bathroom's through there." She pointed down a darkened hallway past a couple passionately dancing together near a wall, their hips pressed together but their mouths and eyes set in a way that seemed like they were also having some sort of serious discussion. Maybe a discussion about politics.

"Cool." Carlos headed in the direction she pointed.

"Is there another one?" Steven asked, making Kingsley jump since he'd completely forgotten the other man was there. "This sand is squirming into too many places."

"Sure," Annika said without hesitation. "Use the one off the master bedroom." She waved Steven toward the same hallway. "And if you want some clothes, just grab some from the cupboard in the bathroom. The green cupboard, not the black."

"Does that mean we have to wait our turn?" Kingsley asked, trying hard *not* to think about showering with Doe Eyes.

He focused instead on how his thin shorts were drying against his skin, making him feel like an alligator with salt water and sand stuck to him. He had another pair of shorts in his bag to change into. While riding over in the van, he'd vaguely thought of going home to shower and change but knew once he went home, he wouldn't want to leave.

"You can do whatever you want," Annika said in response to his question, turning a speculative gaze toward Doe Eyes. "There's an outdoor shower by the pool if you're desperate."

He turned to Doe Eyes. "Are *you* desperate?"

That must have been the cue to leave because Annika turned her back on Kingsley and walked away.

"What did I say?" When Doe Eyes just shook her head, he dismissed the whole thing with a shrug. "How about a drink?"

Now she actually smiled. "Why are you offering me a drink at someone else's house?" There was a hint of nervousness to her words that made him want to gather her close.

"I've been here enough times," he said, trying to pitch his tone to one of reassurance.

She plucked at the hem of the shorts, not looking any less anxious. "I don't even know why I came here with you." White teeth nibbled at her full lower lip.

"Because you enjoy my company, obviously."

Her lip was getting more bruised and soft-looking the more she bit it, and Kingsley was having a hard time keeping his attention away from her mouth. In desperation, he cast his eyes around them, taking in the DJ and competitors he recognized from Hi-Winds who came to Aruba nearly every year. The house was full, and, although he didn't want a drink, he urgently needed something to do with his hands other than wish they were touching a certain tempting woman.

"Let's go grab that drink," he said. "It'll relax you and help take your mind off the whole needing-a-shower thing. At least until Carlos and Steven get out of the bathroom so we can have a turn." She hissed softly in reaction, and he stared down at her. "Get your mind out of the gutter," he said. "I meant our *separate* turns in the bathroom for a shower. If I wanted to invite you for sex, that wouldn't be the way I'd do it." There were a thousand more elegant ways and more convenient places.

"Fine." But she dipped her head, looking anywhere but at him.

Kingsley grinned. "Well, if you do want me to invite you to have a shower with me…"

She shook her head, raising a hand as if she meant to poke him. But her hand dropped as if she realized they weren't quite at that stage of their relationship yet. His grin widened.

At the makeshift bar, he got them both bottles of local beer, then guided her to a narrow and recently vacated space on the sofa that smelled of cigarettes and spilled beer. The impression of being at a college party only grew worse. Funny, he'd been to parties at the house plenty of times and hadn't gotten that vibe. He shifted next to Doe Eyes and wondered what she thought of all this. The music pulsed, warm and mellow, around them.

"So what was it you were talking about with your friend earlier?" she asked, leaning close enough that her breath whispered over his cheek, his mouth.

"I talked about a lot of things," he said.

"You were talking about cigarettes and addiction."

Ah. His mini-confrontation with Carlos in the boat. He wondered why she was even interested in talking about that. It felt like she was latching on to any conversational straw to avoid acknowledging the attraction between them. But he could play if that was what she wanted.

"That's more Carlos's baggage than mine," Kingsley said, then paused before sharing information about his friend that Carlos himself was pretty free with. "He's been in Narcotics Anonymous for a minute, but he replaced drugs with cigarettes. He clings to them thinking that if he gave up cigarettes, then he'd regress to drugs. He goes through a lot of packs in the day."

"That's just replacing one addiction for another. Doesn't seem healthy."

"For him, it's the safest. Everyone has their own way of coping with lesser demons."

As they talked, they leaned more toward each other, and Kingsley didn't realize the sound of the music was rising, getting louder until they were talking practically with their mouths pressed to each other's ears. He lifted the beer to his lips, nodding as they talked about addiction and Carlos and the inherent danger of swimming in the sea at night.

"We don't always need to see where we're going in order to get there," he said. "Sometimes there's a path already charted for us. We just have to head toward our destination and trust."

She turned to him, her mouth damp from her beer bottle. "Are you talking about religion now?"

"I'm talking about life." He looked down at her, watching as she licked away the wetness of the beer but only managed to dampen her lips even more. His own mouth tingled with the urge, ever present now, to kiss her.

"Do you believe in anything?" she asked him.

"Of course. Lots of things." Like the ability of lust to blind him to rational thought and action. With any other woman, he'd already have had her name, maybe even her body spread out in his bed.

She didn't ask him to elaborate on his beliefs or lack thereof; instead she tapped her thumb thoughtfully against her bottom lip. "I believe in making the best choices we can to avoid future pain," she said.

With a nod, he acknowledged the neat way she avoided talking about religion but still managed to reveal something of herself to him, as casual as the revelation had been.

"How about making the best choices to encourage present pleasure?" The way he practically shouted the words in her ear was far from seductive, but he felt her move against him, the press of her thigh against his, skin to skin, growing damp together in the room rapidly filling with people whose very presence battled a too-weak air-conditioning unit.

"Pleasure is fleeting." Her mouth briefly brushed his ear as she spoke, and Kingsley didn't even hide the jolt of desire that moved through him. His mouth opened, and his tongue flicked out to taste the air.

"But it is one of those things that makes this life worth living," he murmured. "I work to keep my family in the style to which it's grown accustomed, but also to afford the things that make me happy. My car, my country club membership, first-class plane tickets to Aruba and everything else I can do to get a certain beautiful woman into my…arms."

He felt her laughter before he heard it, her body shaking with mirth, a bubble of merriment that vibrated off her skin before he heard it just beneath the pounding bass of the music.

"You have very eager arms then," she said.

"You have no idea." He lightly closed his lips around her earlobe as he spoke and heard the soft noise she made despite the loud music.

Kingsley was more than ready to take her to bed.

"King, baby…" A woman stumbled into their private bubble, her knees knocking into his. "Come dance with me." She didn't make it an invitation but a demand, reaching down to grab for his hand.

At his side, Doe Eyes glanced up at the woman, then at him, slowly blinking away the arousal that had clouded her eyes just moments before. Kingsley wanted to see that look on her again.

The woman was a few drinks past drunk, so it was easy for him to slip his hand from hers and refuse what she was offering. "Another time, Chris. Find me later on. I'm trying to close an important deal here."

Chris made a show of pouting, then swished her hips from side to side in her tight skirt. But Kingsley was used to more compelling incentives than that. He shook his head again, and she shrugged before wandering off to find a more willing dance partner.

"You're missing out on a sure thing there," Doe Eyes said when she leaned close to him again.

"That's not what I want tonight," he said.

"What do you want?"

"I think you know."

Again he felt how close to each other they were. The press of her skin against his, bare thigh to bare

thigh, on the sofa that held at least three other people, all minding their own business.

She bit the side of her lips, gaze falling to the beer
bottle clasped in her lap. "We were talking about
choices."

"Were we?"

"Yeah…"

The mood was over. So Kingsley spoke with her
of other things while attraction hummed just beneath
his skin, a steady and thrumming heat that made
him perpetually aware of just how close she was to
him. The volume of the music rose until they were
simply resting their mouths at each other's ears, following the skein of thread in a conversation that was
becoming less and less important.

The smell of marijuana that had been subtle in
the room before grew stronger. A quick glance to
the left confirmed that the man at the far end of the
couch had just lit up a blunt and was offering a hit
to everyone nearby. Kingsley noticed the wrinkling
of the feminine nose next to him.

"You want to relocate?" He jerked his chin toward
the sliding patio doors.

She nodded, nose bumping into the sweat-damp
line of his neck. He couldn't stop the spike of want
that lanced down his belly and directly into his lap.
Kingsley took a quick swallow from his bottle and
stood up. He put out a hand to help her off the couch,
but she was already on her feet and heading past him
toward the door.

He watched her butt, a twitching temptation, for long moments with the taste of beer almost sour in his mouth and the lust rising, hot and steady, in his lap. After subtly adjusting himself, he followed after her through the crowd and slid open the patio doors to escape into the fresh air.

It was cooler outside, but only because of the wind. It howled in the small backyard, where a hammock swayed from the weight of three bodies and the lights were just bright enough to illuminate the dozen or so people in various stages of relaxation, some floating lazily in the pool.

The smell of marijuana still clung to Kingsley's clothes, even outside. He slid the patio door closed behind him, following Doe Eyes toward a recently vacated lawn chair with a footstool beside it. She sat on the footstool, her legs stretched out in front of her.

Kingsley hesitated. "You should take the chair," he said.

"No, thank you." She slipped him an odd smile, then looked around the backyard at the scene that was as familiar to him as any boardroom at Diallo Corporation. The carpet of Astroturf laid down instead of grass that would drink up a whole house worth of water. A stone path leading to the small, round pool in the center of the backyard. Quiet conversation and intimate sounds drifted from the couples and small groups sharing the pool.

At one time, Kingsley would have happily indulged himself in one of these scenes, but not now.

Not with Doe Eyes here. He sank into the lawn chair and calmed his nerves with his second beer of the night.

A sigh came from the beautiful woman near him, and she looked around again with envy in her face. "My mother would never expect me to do something like this."

"Do her expectations matter that much to you?" Kingsley asked.

"I'd like to say no, but I feel like being truthful tonight."

"Truth is a good thing, even between strangers," Kingsley said, intentionally poking at whatever secret it was that she held from him.

She made a noncommittal noise, shrugged and lifted her beer to her lips. Also her second. Someone passing by stumbled into her. With a magician's skill, she held her drink high and away from her body as she tumbled sideways and into Kingsley's knees. He caught her in his arms, instantly aware of the warm sweetness of her, the salt smell in her hair and clothes from their evening in the sea, the scent of beer on her lips.

"Oops! Sorry." The man laughed out his apology as someone else helped him upright, then away from Kingsley and Doe Eyes.

The feel of her against him was a delicious and sensuous weight he didn't want to give up. He could happily hold on to her all night, but she shifted against him, and he helped her sit upright again on her footstool.

"It's a night for missteps," she said.

"Or to loosen the stiffness from your spine." Another sip of beer, another glance across at her.

She licked her lips and turned her bottle around and around between her hands. Kingsley could still feel her against his palms, could still smell the salt and sweat of her skin. He wanted nothing more than to pull her into his lap and taste her, but he didn't reach out. He wanted her to make the first move.

Her eyes, when she raised them to his, were full of conflict. And need. "It's not okay to follow every impulse you have, you know."

"True. But, conversely, not every impulse should be denied."

"How very self-serving of you," she said.

Kingsley smiled in the dark. He'd been called much worse. "And what would be self-serving for you?"

"I'm already here, way past my bedtime. I'm drinking with strangers, and God knows what could happen to me out here."

"The only thing that will happen to you here is what you say you want." He reiterated what he'd told her earlier, meaning every word. His desire for her was a firm and constant thing that ached to be satisfied, but it only demanded satisfaction if she did, too.

When she didn't respond, he put down his beer. "Listen, let me take you home and—"

His words were cut off when she sank into his lap. Her thighs spread over his thighs, feet on the ground, her bottom a round weight in his hands that automatically reached down to cup and bring her close. Her soft arms slid around his neck.

"This is my impulse," she said and kissed him.

Her mouth on his, body settling close, a blanket of heat and passionate goals. But maybe that was him. His intentions rising up to meet whatever it was that she wanted from him.

The kiss was sweet. At least it started off that way. Her breath huffed against his cheek as she turned her head in that age-old choreography of intimacy, her palms sliding up to cup the back of his head. The rake of nails over his scalp, an unexpected sharpness, jerked his hips up, fired pleasure through him and made him abruptly want more. She laughed against his mouth. He licked her lips in answer, gripped her hips and pulled her against him again. Her laughter died as she slid deeper into his lap, the V of her sex flush against his. Her mouth was hot and soft, tongue sliding against his in a way that made him want to take her to bed. *Right damn now.* Kingsley groaned into her mouth.

The sand caught in his clothes rubbed under his shorts and in the vulnerable places under his shirt, making her touch even more potent. He shivered under the smooth caress of her hands down his back, her nails sinking into his shoulders, the press of her bottom in his lap. From just this, kissing, she was going to make him explode.

And he still didn't know her name.

She pressed into him, a ravenous and insistent weight, kissing him like she was devouring something she hadn't had in a very long time. She tasted of beer and sea salt and lust. And Kingsley wanted to drink her all up.

"I like your impulse," he gasped into her mouth as he pushed his hips into hers again.

She hummed and matched him movement for movement, her hips dancing against his in an arousing rhythm, hardening him even more. Her long fingers latched on to his shoulders and her nails dug in deep enough to make him gasp again. She opened up wider for him, and he sucked her tongue, licked every part of her mouth she let him have while his body grew hotter under his clothes. Her fingers dug into his chest through the shirt, then plucked at the buttons, ripping them open. Everything around them disappeared. The people. The music. The right and wrong of what they were doing.

His shirt was open, and her fingers gripped at his skin. The intensity of her desire was merciless, and it brought his want surging up hard and tight. This was no longer some snuggling kitten. She kissed and clawed at him like she wanted to consume him, and he matched the pace of her movements, of her wants, gasping into her mouth as their bodies twisted together.

She yanked her mouth away from his, and Kingsley growled again, this time in disappointment. What he'd done was too much. This wasn't what she wanted from him, and he opened his mouth to apologize. But the apology became a grunt when her lips locked onto the side of his neck, her teeth on his skin, her fingernails raking over his bare nipples and the heated skin of his chest. A firestorm of pleasure exploded in his belly.

Kingsley gripped the hair at the back of her head, pressing her mouth harder into his skin. "Do that again," he groaned into her ear.

She pinched his nipple and bit him again, and Kingsley's hips surged up, once, then twice, mimicking what he wanted to do with her. The lawn chair groaned underneath them. The breeze brushed cool and lush over the wetness left by her mouth as she dipped lower to suck and bite more of his throat. Another long and low grown left Kingsley's throat. He wouldn't be able to last much longer. His heartbeat pounded in his chest. The blood rushed through him fast, and faster. He gasped and held on to her hips grinding rhythmically down on him. He was going to lose it right now, and there was nothing he wanted to do to stop it.

With his fingers tangled in her loose hair, Kingsley opened his mouth to gasp her name, realized he didn't know it and hissed out a curse instead.

"You're killing me!" He moaned when her hand closed over him through his shorts.

"Not yet." Then she bit down on his nipple again, apparently oblivious to his friends, who'd drifted out of the crowd to watch Kingsley damn near explode in her hand.

Chapter 4

"I think I won that bet."

The voice—Carlos's—from too close made Adah jerk her mouth away from Kingsley's chest. She tried to pull completely away, but Kingsley followed with his mouth, panting. She kept him back with a hand pressed against his chest and felt the hard and unsteady beat of his heart, the firmness of his bare muscles. Embarrassment and residual desire flushed her from head to toe.

Carlos emerged from the otherwise anonymous crowd, beer in hand, along with Annika, who was smoking a cigarette.

When Adah had chosen this spot to sit, it had been the most private place on the patio. Everyone else had been situated by the pool or near the wide concrete slab of the patio. But the area had quickly become swarmed with people, and—her cheeks flushed with embarrassment at the thought—she hadn't cared when she'd climbed in Kingsley's lap to kiss him.

She turned back into the conversation happening near her in time to hear Annika say, "You didn't win anything yet. They aren't having sex. That's just kissing."

They were talking about her and Kingsley. She flushed again and felt the firm touch of his hand at the small of her back trying to keep her in his lap.

"Let me up," she said, scrambling away from him.

Adah was almost disappointed at how quickly Kingsley let her go, hands falling away to grip the sides of the chair. His eyes were deep pools of swirling emotion. Want and eagerness, his mouth wet from their kisses, his chest heaving under the press of her hand. She drew her hand back as if burned, not realizing that she'd still been touching him even as she fought to get away.

She didn't know what had gotten into her. Making out in public with a near stranger wasn't something she ever did. She hadn't drunk that many beers; she wasn't that tired. But she remembered the sweet twine of the smoke from the people who had sat near them inside the house. Yes. It had to be that. A contact high making her act in a way she normally wouldn't.

"I need to go," she said.

She could still feel him on her mouth, tingling and warm, the desire pooling her lap, leaving her molten and needy. And frightened. Adah dragged the back of her hand over her damp mouth and thought she saw a flash of hurt in Kingsley's eyes before he lowered them.

She tugged the edges of her unbuttoned shirt closed over obviously hard nipples and stood on shaky legs, trying to control her breathing and the desire rippling through her that even now pulled her back toward him. His taste was still in her mouth. She swallowed it.

"I need to leave here," she said again and started toward the path curving around the side of the house to the front yard, fully intending to walk back to her hotel. The island was small. It couldn't be that far away. She vaguely heard Annika and Carlos talking with Kingsley, then the sound of his sure footfalls behind her,

"I'll take you home," he said when he caught up. "It's not safe for you to walk at night by yourself."

But she kept going. It felt too dangerous to be with *him*. If it hadn't been for the interruption, she didn't know how far she'd have taken it. Kissing him had felt so damn good. She'd been moments away from begging him to slip her panties to the side and slam their bodies together. She nearly groaned at the thought.

"What am I doing?" she muttered out loud.

Kingsley grabbed her, and she whirled around to

face him, ready to tell him to go to hell. But his hand left her arm as quickly as it landed.

"My truck is that way." He pointed toward the left and a sandy strip of a path leading away from the main road where the van had taken them earlier. The road was well lit and a pair of large dogs, one white and the other golden brown, settled themselves under a nearby tree and watched Adah with glowing eyes. She flinched away from the dogs and dropped back until she was walking a little behind Kingsley, prepared to use his body as a shield if they attacked.

"You don't have to be afraid," he said, his voice soft and much too close. "I won't let them bite you."

He sounded confident, but her experience with dogs had taught her how unpredictable they were. A neighborhood dog had bitten her sister when they were toddlers, and she never forgot it. The growling menace of the dog, the blood on Zoe's leg, the trip to the hospital and the shots she'd had to get afterward. Keeping a close eye on the nearby dogs, Adah gripped her arms to stop herself from reaching out and grabbing on to Kingsley like a frightened child.

"It's this one." He led her toward a fenced front yard.

The house behind the low white fence was small and narrow. Smaller than the two-story house they'd just left behind with its sprawling single level, lights on in the drive, and farther back, a high wooden fence closing off the backyard from view. Details of deep green exterior walls, a wooden front door and a nearby garden of tall cacti emerged in the dark.

An older-model truck stood small and silent in the front yard, and a set of keys jangled. "You can get in," Kingsley said. "It's open."

The passenger door opened with a squeak of its hinges, and Adah climbed in, immediately rolling down the windows to release some of the heat trapped inside. Kingsley started the truck after a single glance at her.

"Where am I going?"

She told him the name of the hotel.

"That's a far walk," he said. "You would still be walking come sunrise."

"I'm faster than I look," she said.

His smile flashed. "I don't doubt it."

Moonlight glinted off the curve of his mouth and revealed again the muscled flesh beneath his mostly unbuttoned shirt. Adah took deliberate and deep breaths to stop herself from crawling into his lap again. This was getting ridiculous.

Kingsley started the truck and put it in gear. It rumbled over the rock gravel of the driveway, rolling out into the street with a full-throated growl. Silence swayed between them with each movement of the truck down the paved road.

Although it was mostly dark, Adah could see his hand work the gearshift, a commanding and sexy manipulation of the vehicle that vividly recalled the feeling of his hands on her. She shifted in the seat and looked away from his strong, thick-veined hand. With the shuddering breath she took, Adah could practically smell the arousal wafting up from between her own thighs.

She cleared her throat. "I'm sorry for what happened back there."

He looked at her. "Are you? Why?"

"Because…" *I'm practically engaged.* "Because we just met. It was inappropriate." She winced at how like her mother she sounded. And of all the times to be thinking of her mother…

"There's nothing inappropriate or wrong about what we did. Nobody forced you to sit in my lap, and there sure as hell wasn't a gun to my head when I grabbed your ass like it was mine." He playfully leered at her. "I'm into you. And I'm reasonably sure you like me. It's all perfectly normal."

Adah made a sound of frustration. Of course, it would seem fine to someone like him. He probably had women lined up every place he went. She was just the one weirdo who basically dared herself to go to a party with him, then, while potentially under the influence of a contact marijuana high, practically had sex with him in public. No, this wasn't at all a "normal" thing for her.

"Enjoyment is not all that determines whether or not something is wrong or right," she finally settled on saying.

"It's a good place to start, though," he countered.

This conversation felt far too familiar, like they'd

already discussed pleasure and its larger meaning before. How could she have recurring topics of conversation with a guy she just met? She shook her head
at the foolishness of it all.

"This is my hotel," she called out with relief when
she saw the familiar archway just outside her hotel's parking lot. But Kingsley was already turning
into the palm-tree-lined driveway, obviously familiar
with where he was. The lot was full, an indication
of how popular the locale was, especially during the
summer high season. It was a great combination of
luxurious and intimate with its four-star reputation
and homey feel. The long and wide front veranda
was one of the things that had made her love it at
first sight. From now on, though, she was going to
adore it a little less. The woman sitting on the veranda watched the truck with an intensity that was
obvious even from so far away.

Fighting a blush of embarrassment, Adah sighed
under her breath and opened the truck's door, aware
of both Kingsley sitting silently beside her and of the
woman curled up on one of the chairs on the veranda.

"Mother, what are you doing up so late?"

Her mother, draped in an oversize scarf and bun-
dled up against the late evening breeze, sat on one
of the rattan chairs, looking nearly half asleep but
prepared to wait there all night.

"I could ask you the same question."

Or you could not. Adah opened her mouth to tell
her mother just how much of a grown woman she

was, one who could stay out all night if she chose. But her mother looked away from her and toward Kingsley, who climbed out of the truck just then.

She flicked her gaze to the side to look at him and bit her lip. There was nothing she could say in her defense. Kingsley looked like he'd been mauled by a wildcat. Or had been rolling around in bed with one. His shirt was unbuttoned halfway down his chest to show claw marks over his pecs and around his nipples; the board shorts sat low on his narrow hips to emphasize his undeniable maleness.

The breath left her mother in an audible hiss, like air from a deflating tire. "Young man, you should be ashamed of yourself for carrying on with an engaged woman."

"Mother!"

They both stared at her.

"What?" Her mother looked at her with disappointment and a hint of anger around her elegant mouth. "We don't do things like this, Adah. We just don't." Adah noticed Kingsley's twitch at the sound of her name. But she couldn't pay attention to that now.

But I'm not engaged, she wanted to shout. *I haven't agreed to anything yet.*

Kingsley nodded like a puzzle piece had finally fallen into place. "You're engaged," he said. It was a statement, not a question. Like he'd known all along.

"Yes, she is," her mother answered for her. "And

you should leave her alone. This is not very noble of either of you."

Kingsley winced. "Don't worry, ma'am. If I'd known about her engagement, I wouldn't have let things get this far."

Her mother's gaze swung to Adah and over her figure as if she could see the events of the night imprinted on her. "*This far?* What does that mean exactly?"

Adah cursed under her breath. She wanted to touch Kingsley in reassurance, to let him know she hadn't hidden an engagement from him, that this wasn't about blatant infidelity or something equally repulsive. But he was stepping away from her, abandoning the pose of protection he'd taken on once out of the truck. Like he was finished with her. Something in Adah's chest squeezed painfully.

"I'll see you around…Adah." Kingsley spoke her name like a stranger, like the Doe Eyes he'd known and caressed had disappeared completely, leaving an unknown and unappealing woman in her place. After a nod to her mother, he climbed back into the truck. He was gone before Adah could think of what to say to him.

"What were you thinking?" Her mother stood up. What should have been a threat looked like defeat in her. Lines dragged down the corners of her mouth; her eyes looked haunted.

Oh God. Adah pressed the heels of her hands into her eyes. She wanted to just sink through the floor.

Her mother's disappointment was a heavy thing, unwieldy. Something she was tired of bearing.

This time, though, she knew she deserved it. She'd taken Kingsley up on the invitation to go snorkeling understanding that it had the possibility of leading to more, knowing that her blood turned to fire in her veins at just one look from him. Even if nothing had happened between them in the water or during the course of the night, it would only be a matter of time before she gave in to her attraction to him. And, at the back of her mind, she'd thought it would be worth it. A night of exquisite recklessness in exchange for apologizing profusely for her bad behavior. But looking into the face of her mother's disappointment made her doubt the value of the exchange.

"I thought you wanted to marry Bennett," Thandie said. She adjusted the shawl around her shoulders, pulling it tightly. Like Adah's bad decision had chilled her in a way the night's brisk breeze hadn't been able to. "Everything is already set for this marriage," she said, as if she couldn't imagine putting a stop to what had been put into motion for her daughter and for her company. A sacrifice of one and the rescue of the other.

"Mother, I want to help you and Daddy. I really do." Adah wrapped her arms around her own waist, holding tight to stop herself from flying apart. She barely stopped the "but" from leaving her lips. "I'm tired, Mother." Adah sighed and took a step toward the front door.

"Is that all you have to say?" Thandie asked; then her look changed. She stepped closer. "Are you okay? That man didn't do anything to you, did he?"

"No, no. He didn't. He was perfect." She bit her lip, afraid of whatever else she might say about Kingsley and the time they'd spent together. "We can talk tomorrow."

Finally giving in to the urge for escape, Adah walked into the hotel. She didn't remember getting in the elevator or going to her room. She didn't recall taking a shower and getting into bed, but soon she lay huddled under the covers with her hair wet and plastered to the back of her neck and to her cheek. She stared at the chair across from her bed overcrowded with clothes, and she felt the messiness was reflective of her life.

"I need to get it together."

She didn't know if it was tears or water from her wet hair that slipped down her cheeks. But in the end, it didn't really matter. The feeling was the same.

The sound of her ringing phone jolted her out of a dream that was all water, a slippery eel sliding over her arms and belly, stinging her with sweet jolts of electricity that pulled her farther and farther down into the sea. She was happy, her body more alive than it had ever been even as she sank to certain underwater death. The eel tightened its grip around her thighs and her waist, and its tender hold on her throat threatened pleasure more than anything else. She awoke with a gasp, jerking her head up, her body floating out of sleep like she was surfacing from a dive.

"Hello?" She didn't look at the glowing screen of the phone to see who it was.

"Girl, are you okay?"

The remnants of the dream evaporated with the sound of her friend's voice on the other end of the line.

"Selene?" The last she'd seen of her had been at the Atlanta airport, dropping her off and wishing Adah clarity to decide what to do about this marriage she'd agreed to before she'd known any better.

"You said you'd Messenger or WhatsApp me when you got in. I gave you a day to get it together, but now you're just inconsiderate." Her friend's accent was sweet as sugar, but when she was pissed, every word could burn like acid.

Adah muttered a curse. "Sorry! My mind's been..." She didn't even know what else to say about her state of mind.

"You don't have to tell me how your brains are more scrambled than a platter of Waffle House hash browns, but what you do have to do is let me know you weren't killed by some roving maniac on that damn island."

Chastised, Adah sighed and subsided back into the sheets. "I'm sorry. I'm safe."

"The first part I'm sure of, but what about the second? I heard your mama took off after you as soon as she found out you left town." Adah opened her mouth to ask the obvious, but Selene just kept going. "Before you ask foolish questions, I'll just go ahead and say I was *not* the one who told her where you went."

Adah rolled back to the center of the bed and sat up, propping herself up on the overstuffed pillows. "It doesn't really matter anyway. She's here—"

"And making trouble?"

"And making things even harder than before. I already wasn't sure about what I promised, but now she's just pushing me more and more in that direction. And the more she pushes, the more I want to resist." Suddenly Adah felt her throat close up, her eyes burning with tears.

"But there's more, right?" Selene asked. She seemed to know Adah better than she knew herself some days. Their time going to the same schools and living in the same city all their lives only reinforced their bond and sometimes uncanny knowledge of each other.

"I met someone."

"Are you fu—" Selene stopped. "You've been down there for less than two days. How are you gonna meet a man when you're supposed to be working on your own damn issues?"

"I got lucky?" Adah made sure her tone conveyed the very opposite.

"Let me guess, your mama found out about your

island stud and now she thinks you're deliberately setting out to ruin the company and the family name at the same time."

"She didn't do it on purpose, but you know how focused she can be sometimes. It's not malicious."

"Damn, girl."

"I know."

At times Adah felt like a walking symbol of everything her parents had lost when her sister died. Someone smarter, more vibrant and willing to sacrifice herself for the good of the family. Zoe wouldn't have hesitated when it came to marrying Bennett. She would've seen it as her duty and her privilege. But now the responsibility fell to Adah, who felt conflicted by the desire for a life she shouldn't want. Her cowardice and lack of commitment to anything other than her wish not to be tied down made her feel weak.

True, she hadn't taken a lover since committing to the marriage. Instead she'd focused her energies on building the boutique day care service that had become her passion. She'd cultivated her friendships, traveled to more than a dozen countries, enjoyed everything life had to offer that had nothing to do with sex. But all those years of self-denial were catching up with her. Lust for Kingsley had swept her out of her mind and right into his lap. She licked her lips, and although she tasted only sleep, she imagined a hint of him still rested on her tongue.

"Your mama can be scary," Selene said, bringing her back from the memory of Kingsley in her mouth.

Adah laughed, a rough and unhappy sound. "She isn't. Not really."

She could practically hear the shrug on the other end of the line. Selene knew it was fear of disappointing Thandie rather than fear of anything she would do or say that had kept Adah in line for so long. She sighed.

"I just don't know what to do." Adah climbed out of bed, wiping a hand across her face. "I'm just stuck in this strange I-don't-know phase. It's like I'm in high school all over again."

A rustling came through the phone line, Selene probably rummaging through her fancy closet for clothes to wear during her ridiculously early workout. "What do you want to do?"

"I want to run away," Adah whined.

"You already tried that, and your mama and all your worries just followed you down there."

Now Adah wanted to swear and throw things. "You're right." She stumbled to the bathroom to rinse the sleep from her mouth and peer at herself in the mirror. Hair in a bird's nest, face puffy from sleep, a look of hopelessness pulling down the sides of her mouth.

"What should I do, Selene?"

"Honey, you already know what to do. You just don't want to do it."

Adah stuck her tongue out at her reflection in the mirror, pretending it was Selene. "You're not being helpful." She started brushing her teeth.

"Oh, please. I'm just not giving you an easy out." Sounds of more productivity came from the other end of the line. Adah imagined the muffled thump was one of Selene's expensive pots against her tiled countertop. "Speaking of what to do, I hope you don't think Bennett has been as faithful to your premarriage as you've been."

"I don't expect him to be." Adah said the words around her toothbrush and the white foam from the toothpaste building up in her mouth.

Although Bennett was one of the few reliable and much-loved men in Adah's life, he and Selene didn't have much to do with each other. They seemed to orbit Adah's existence in two separate directions, connecting very rarely.

"You should," Selene said about Bennett's apparent infidelity. "He is your soon-to-be fiancé after all." She made a disapproving noise, sounding just like Thandie in a way she wouldn't have liked one bit if Adah pointed it out. "Although no one in town would believe it since he's so very discreet, that man has been petting every peach between here and the Mason-Dixon Line."

Adah laughed and almost choked on her toothbrush. "How do you even know that?"

"What? I didn't understand a word you just said."

Adah spat out her toothpaste and repeated her question.

"I have eyes, honey, and so does Blake." Unlike Adah and Selene, their friend Blake was happily married and had a baby on the way. She wasn't around these days as much as before she got married, but she was still an integral part of their trio. "She saw him at the High Museum with a girl who was hanging all over him. Later that night, she swore up and down that she saw them step into one of the closets for a quickie."

Adah giggled. "Damn, is she stalking him now?" She wasn't surprised by her lack of jealousy at hearing the news of Bennett's very active sex life. Sometimes she wanted to care more about his hypothetical infidelities, but the stories her friends told her about his antics only made her laugh. Yes, she felt vaguely scandalized by those stories but she also wanted to hear more, impressed by the set of brass ones he must have to get away with half the things he did.

"Not stalking. She just cares about you, just like I do," Selene said.

"I know…" Adah stuck the phone between her cheek and shoulder to smooth argon oil and leave-in conditioner in her hair.

Over the years Bennett had become more of a brother to her than a fiancé. Even a *potential* fiancé. They talked every now and then, both over the phone and in person during epic three-hour lunches, sometimes about their intended future together but most times not. He was easygoing and utterly confident as only the sole child and privileged son of relatively well-off Southern parents could be.

He loved women and sailing. After college, he'd borrowed a boat from one of his Exeter classmates and sailed around the world on his own, stopping wherever he felt like and staying however long he desired just because he wanted the solitude and the challenge. Sometimes Adah felt jealous of him being able and willing to do anything he wanted without worrying about his parents' disappointment or disapproval. Maybe he would understand what she was going through.

"So are you going to talk to him?" Selene reached into Adah's mind and plucked the thought right out of it.

"I think I need to."

"And what are you going to say?"

"Why are you asking me questions I don't know the answers to?" She turned and left the bathroom.

Selene laughed at her. "Girl…"

"I know."

After Adah hung up, she felt a lot better. She took her morning shower and went out to the balcony to make the inevitable phone call. Cell phone in hand, she sat on one of the two reclining chairs and looked down on the sand and the stretch of blue water shimmering like diamonds under the sun.

She was second-guessing her decision to call Bennett when the phone rang.

"I hear you're already getting yourself in trouble down there in Aruba." Bennett's voice rumbled through the phone.

She drew in a breath of surprise, and happiness.

Unlike the quiet domesticity of Selene's surroundings, she could hear the chaos of a bar wherever Bennett was. Thudding dance music and the sound of laughter, high and manic, that came at the height of a night's debauch. She looked at the phone in amazement.

"Isn't it eight o'clock in the morning?" she asked.

"It's five o'clock somewhere," he said with laughter in his deep voice. "Besides, I'm not in Atlanta. And don't try to change the subject. What's up with you?"

The music faded away even more. Adah heard the bang of a door closing, then the quiet murmur of voices. She blew out a breath of air. "What do you know?"

"Selene called me. She said you might need to talk."

Adah frowned. She didn't think Selene and Bennett knew each other well enough to have each other's phone numbers. Thinking back to the conversation she'd had earlier with her best friend, she tried to think of anything Selene had said that would hint at some sort of friendship with Bennett.

Through the phone, he made a tut-tut sound.

"Don't get distracted yourself either. I called you on a mission."

Adah choked on a laugh. Sometimes she thought he knew her better than he ought to. Unpredictable but unfailingly kind and generous, Bennett was the kind of man most women dreamed of. She wished she could jump in and commit to him like their parents wanted. There were worse men out there.

But she didn't think those reasons were enough for her to marry him.

"Tell me," he prodded when she was quiet too long.

Adah took a breath. "I'm not sure this marriage thing is for us."

"It worked out fine for our parents," he said. "Don't be so cynical." There was humor in his soft drawl, a warm invitation to tell him everything on her mind.

"What if this is a mistake?" She heard the quiver in her voice, but it was too late to take back the whining uncertainty of her declaration.

"This is only a mistake if you allow it to be. Do you want something else?"

Adah shook her head although an image of Kingsley immediately came into her mind. "I want to be sure."

Bennett didn't hesitate. "Then take your time to be sure. Our parents can wait. This is our lives, not theirs."

Adah swallowed. It would have been much easier to break off the agreement if she didn't like Bennett so much and if he wasn't such a damn nice guy. A good man who would make a great husband some-day. *For someone else.* The words crept into her con-sciousness and wouldn't be silenced.

She dropped her head back and pressed the heel of a hand over her closed eye.

"It's not that simple," she said.

"As usual, you're overthinking, but far be it from me to deprive you of one of your favorite pastimes." His laugh was soft and warm though it was just a breath from being mocking.

"Just relax on your island, Adah. Go swimming. Make love with a handsome stranger—" she nearly choked "—and when you're completely liquid and sitting in the seat of who you are, your mind and heart will know what to do. Stop making a bigger deal of it than it is."

She didn't have to make a big deal out of this. This was *already* a huge issue, even if he was blasé enough to ignore the ramifications of what she was contemplating. But Adah took a cue from him, drew a breath deep into her lungs and slowly released it.

"Okay."

He laughed then. She pictured him standing on top of one of his beloved rooftop bars or clubs in some country she'd never been to, the nighttime city spread out below him, aglow with light.

"That's all you have to say?" he asked. "Just okay?"

"What else is there? You don't have my parents—at least not yet—so you don't know how trying to get away from their expectations is like struggling to crawl out from under an avalanche. It's nearly impossible."

"I believe in you, baby girl."

She shook her head finally, unable to deal with his blind optimism. "I'll talk with you later, Bennett."

"All right. Let me know how it works out."

"You'll be one of the first to know," she said with a twist of her lips.

"Oh yeah. Right." He laughed again, careless and carefree, as if whether or not to choose to go ahead with their marriage wouldn't affect him in the least. "Take it easy, baby girl. We'll talk soon."

Adah wandered back into the room, thinking about what Bennett and Selene had told her. And she thought about Kingsley's face the last time she'd seen him, the flinch in his eyes when her mother told him she was engaged. The beginnings of a headache throbbed above her left eye.

After a shower and properly seeing to her hair, Adah left the hotel, deliberately being quiet so as not to disturb her mother. Although she wouldn't have called it "sneaking out." Not really.

She had a decision to make, but before then she urgently had an apology to give.

Although at the best of times Adah was absent-minded, she actually had an excellent sense of direction. The ride from the party had been distracting, to say the least, with Kingsley a temptation to her senses and her apparently loose sense of morality. But between taking peeks at his body unself-consciously bared by the open buttons of his shirt, she'd also looked at the landmarks they'd passed, taking note of everything around her. She called a taxi to take her to the entrance of the modest community in the hills where she was 90 percent certain Kingsley lived.

It didn't take her long to find his house, a single-story building with a narrow facade and, as confirmation that she was in the right place, a solitary older-model truck in its front yard. It was early, barely nine o'clock, but she assumed he would be home.

Her feet crunched in the gravel as she approached the house, nibbling on her lip and trying to think of the best way to tell him she was sorry for…everything. Well, maybe not exactly *everything*. She was about to knock on the door when the sound of a warning yip yanked her gaze to the road just in front of the house. It was the two dogs from the evening before. This time they had two more dogs with them, both bigger. Their tongues hung out in the morning heat as they eyed her with uncertain intent.

Adah shrank back on the veranda, looking around. There was no one else on the street, just her and the dogs, who seemed resolved to walk into Kingsley's front yard. Her heart started a panicked beat in her chest. She gripped the railing and backed away from the dogs.

Damn!

They came closer, sniffing vaguely at one another, then at the air in front of their noses while watching Adah, like they were making a game of it and stalking her. Adah didn't think. She jumped over the railing of the veranda and took off toward the nearest escape from the dogs. The gate leading to the backyard. She grabbed the handle and rattled it, cursing when it refused to open, practically feeling the dogs' hot breath on her heels. Panting in fear, she gripped the top of the fence and levered herself over, yelping when one of her sandals fell off.

She landed on the other side of the fence with a gasp. Her knees jerked from the landing, and gravel dug into the bottom of her naked foot. But she was safe. She leaned back against the fence with her eyes closed and her palms flat against the warm board of the fence.

"This is unexpected."

Her eyes flew open at the sound of Kingsley's voice.

She almost squeezed them shut again. Kingsley was lying by the side of his pool, his gorgeous skin spread out and glistening under the sun, absolutely naked. Adah swallowed hard and pressed her fingernails into the wooden fence at her back.

"I promise you I didn't do this on purpose." She tried to look everywhere but at his body, but her eyes drifted down from his face with each passing moment she looked in his direction. Finally Adah settled for staring at the empty space just to the left of his jaw.

"The dogs, right?"

He sounded amused, and although she wasn't looking—she really wasn't—she saw him sit up from the chair and put aside a stack of official-looking papers. "They can be a little scary," he said.

She thought he was going to grab a towel to cover himself, but he only braced his elbows on widespread knees to give her his undivided attention. Adah licked her suddenly dry lips. Since it would be idiotic to tell the man to put on clothes when he was clearly relaxing in his own backyard, where she was trespassing, she settled for standing up straight against the fence and tried to look more at ease, straightening her knees and taking subtle deep breaths, trying not to ogle him. He was making it very, very hard.

Adah cleared her throat. "I came to apologize about last night."

For a moment he said nothing, made no motion. Then he stood and walked toward the pool. She took a breath of relief when he sank beneath the surface of the water, inch by inch, his legs, feet, calves, the narrow hips and... Adah yanked her eyes up to his face but got distracted by the muscled planes of his chest and the faint marks from her fingernails she saw there. She felt him smile before she saw the curving amusement of his mouth.

"What part of last night are you here to apologize for, *Adah*?"

Adah flushed and watched as he swam lazily to the deep end, the water covering him all the way to his chest and splashing at the edges of the pool.

With him safely on the other side of the yard, she came closer, skirting the pool to perch next to the chair he'd just abandoned.

"There is a lot to apologize for," she said, thinking of the kiss she'd initiated without full disclosure of her circumstances. "I'm sorry I put you in that awkward position. It was selfish. And I should've known better. I do know better. I was just…" She trailed off, not knowing how much to reveal of what had been tearing her apart. "I'm sorry."

For a long moment, he looked at her, steady-eyed and handsome, the sun sparkling off the water gilding his face and throat. It didn't seem fair that all she wanted to do was slink closer to him and kiss his face all over, tease his mouth with her tongue and touch him until every anxiety she had simply disappeared, leaving just him and her and the sun and whatever could blossom between them. But Aruba wasn't a place to plant seeds, and this was not what she had come to him for.

"Tell me," he said, as he tread water in the deep end of the pool. "What exactly are you sorry for? Tell me. Explicitly."

He rolled the last word in his mouth in a way that made her want to drop to her knees in front of him, risk drowning in the pool to give in to every temptation he presented. And he knew exactly what he was doing. The way he watched her, eyes unrelenting and hard, said as much.

She had to open her mouth and start speaking twice to finally get the words out. "I made a mess of my life." Adah chewed the corner of her lip until it felt raw. "There's an arrangement that was made a long time ago. I agreed to it. Marriage." The last word felt like it curdled in Adah's mouth. "I shouldn't have kissed you."

"And now you're here for…?"

More. "To throw myself at your abundant mercy?" She tipped her head at him in question, repentant and almost willing to grovel for his forgiveness and whatever else he wanted to give.

Kingsley was too beautiful, floating in the water just out of arm's reach. Despite what Bennett had said, this wasn't easy. There was no decision for her to make. Her course was set, and there was nothing she could do about it except minimize the people she hurt before she acquiesced to the inevitable. She pursed her lips at Kingsley while he floated in the water and seemingly pondered her prostration.

Then finally he said, "My…mercy is nothing if not abundant. Despite what I wanted when we met, we can be friends instead. I'm not a slave to my penis. It's fun to pretend that I am, but—" He grinned, warm and teasing as the frost melted from his gaze. "I control the thing more than it controls me."

She felt an answering smile twitch across her face. With deep relief, she leaned all the way back in the chair, feeling an unspoken permission to look at him now. A mistake. He was waist deep in the pool, water dripping down his face and neck to sparkle in the sprinkling of hair on his chest and the dark trail dragging her eyes down. Adah drew in more air through her nose and felt her thoughts scatter like marbles across a slippery tile floor, a cacophony of color, noise and frustrated intent. Why was she so helpless to his charms?

She liked to think she'd known men more attractive than Kingsley. But she couldn't recall a single one. Bennett was very attractive. When she'd offered to take one for the team by becoming his pre-fiancée, she thought she was getting a pretty good deal. But that first look at Kingsley on the beach, floating above her head with his bared chest and focused attention, and she'd felt a full burst of lust that took her completely by surprise. She was used to denying herself, though, so it had been nothing to walk away from him. Now it was difficult to follow that routine. Nearly impossible. But, like Kingsley had said, maybe she could keep him in her life as a friend.

She cleared her throat again and dragged her eyes from what they were desperately trying to see below the water line. "Okay. That's good. That was all I wanted. To apologize and make sure you weren't put off by the things my mother said last night."

"Mothers have said worse to me." He winked at her.

Adah shook her head, a smile teased out of her and into the early afternoon despite herself.

"Would you like to stay for breakfast?" he asked, swimming closer. "Friends do that—right? Have breakfast together?"

She tried not to think of the exact circumstances where she'd love to have breakfast with him—but the images came hot and fast—sweat, sex, the groaning pleasure of him on top of her, inside her. Then after, a light breakfast in bed, him feeding her luscious red strawberries, before pulling her down into the sheets to wear her out again. Adah dipped her head to press a burning cheek into the relative coolness of her shoulder.

"I wish I could," she said. "But I have to go." *Before I do something I should regret.* She stood up, brushing off the back of her shorts. "Enjoy your swim. I'm sure I'll see you again."

"I am, too," he said, his tone low and teasing. "If you want to take the initiative, know you're welcome to visit me here anytime you like."

"Um…thanks." She would definitely not be taking him up on that invitation.

"Are you on the island for much longer?" Kingsley asked the question just as she turned away.

More than enough time to get in trouble with you again. "Another five days," she said. "Not much more time."

"Good to know," he said. "I'll see you soon. *Friend.*"

The word was loaded with sensuality. And that both frightened and excited her.

She rolled her eyes at her own idiocy. *Get a grip, girl!*

"See you around, Kingsley."

Chapter 5

He still wanted her.

Kingsley finished the reports his assistant had suckered him into reviewing before leaving for the beach and his freestyle kite-surfing event at Hi-Winds. Adah stayed in his mind the entire time. The way she'd looked jumping over his fence, chest heaving with fear as she glanced over her shoulder toward the no longer visible pack of dogs. And when she'd seen him, it was like she was facing the dogs all over again, her face twisted in shock.

She wasn't for him, this woman who couldn't give him any of what he wanted.

But he still wanted.

On the beach the sun was at the perfect height,

and the morning winds pawed at his skin, warm and friendly. He had loved taking part in the long-distance kiting the day before, a chance to skim across the sea and sky with friends and competitors he hadn't seen in a year or so. But today was his favorite event. He had to beat his friends to take home the money and the trophy. The $5,000 prize money didn't impress him. He had that much in his spending cash for the week. It was the physical challenge of the kite and the water, the pull on his muscles and on his senses, adrenaline sparking through his body like sex, and the view like no other.

Kingsley prepped for his event, stretching and curling his toes in the hot sand as he watched the water, where his closest competitor performed a reverse somersault and landed upright. The crowd cheered, wild and congratulatory. *Yeah.* He needed to get his head in the game and off Adah.

When it was his turn, everything in him focused on controlling the parachute in the air and keeping the board balanced. He was all in. His body responded like it was meant to, breath controlled, the shock of landing on the water reverberating through the kite board and into his knees. His breath rushed out.

Yes.

He harnessed the wind under his parachute again and flew up. One breath in, then *higher*. Muscles tight. The sweat pouring off him, seawater salting his lips and tongue, and then launched into the double flip he'd been practicing all week. Breath out. The shock of the landing. Applause. Kingsley grinned as he sailed across the water, then up into the air as the wind came back for him, maneuvering him neatly above the shimmering water close to the beach, the deeper blue as impenetrable as a certain woman's gaze. And he slipped, looking over the gathered crowd to see if *she* was there.

But no. A beach full of pale bodies. No Adah. His arm twitched, and he felt himself losing control of the kite, his body jerking hard in the air as the wind pushed him farther out and away from any possible sighting of Adah. He had to get his mind off her.

Kingsley drew in a hard breath and got back to business. A flash of pale under the water caught his eye—a shark—and he frowned, tightening his grip on the kite straps and fighting the instinctive surge of panic. Now he had another reason to keep his head in the game. He landed on the surface with a splash, grunted when the kite tugged at his harness. He yanked the brake line, feeling the answering roll in his shoulder muscles, the flexing and undulations of his back as he got the kite closer to the beach.

Max, one of the guys who'd gone up before him, grabbed the leading edge of the kite and guided it to the sand while Kingsley kicked off the board to the renewed applause of people watching.

"That was cool! I didn't know you perfected that triple flip you almost killed yourself over last year." Max offered up a fist bump. "Nice going."

"Thanks!" Although it hadn't been a necessary part of the competition, Kingsley had obsessed about pulling off the triple. He'd damn near fallen on his head a few times while he was practicing it. But out on the water, it had felt effortless, a symphony of his muscles and breath working together to produce one of the best moves he'd ever done. Now that the challenge was met, what was next? A thought of Adah flashed in his mind.

"Good luck out there, Max. The wind is nice, but I spotted a shark. Far out but still there."

Max cursed. "Those things freak me out."

"You're not the only one," Kingsley muttered.

When he'd seen the shark, a cold fear had come over him. It wasn't his first time seeing one while up in a kite, and he didn't want this to be his first time getting bitten by one. He preferred his limbs right where they were, attached to his body.

"You were really great out there."

A trio of women walked up to Kingsley. Max gave him a look before lifting his hand in a wave.

"See you later, man." He seemed to enjoy the bikini-clad backsides of the girls as he walked away, grinning and giving Kingsley the thumbs-up behind their backs.

Kingsley accepted the compliment from the women with gracious thanks and continued rolling up his kite. He felt their eyes on him, all three of them, hungry like the shark he'd managed to avoid in the water.

"We'd love to buy you a drink," one of them said.

They were all pretty, dressed in colorful bikinis that showed off their shapes and newly acquired tans. It didn't seem like one was trying to get him more than the others; instead all three women seemed intent on pursuing him. He hadn't been offered a foursome in a long time. Kingsley thought about Adah and the flash of her eyes, her soft body and the fit of her hand in his while they were snorkeling together.

"Sure," he said. "Where do you have in mind?"

He was a single and completely available man. He didn't have a wife or girlfriend to stop him from taking these women up on whatever it was they were offering.

"There's a bar at the Sundowner." A hotel not too far away. "They have great drinks and big beds." The third one spoke up now, the curviest of her friends, with a tilted mouth that reminded Kingsley a bit of Adah. He clenched his jaw tight. He didn't need to think about her. She was as good as married and off-limits.

"Okay. Why not?"

He exchanged numbers with the women and agreed to meet them at the hotel bar that night. The rest of the tournament was an exercise in frustration. He alternately congratulated and criticized himself for agreeing to meet the women for what was guaranteed to be a confusing foursome. But he couldn't have Adah. Not in the way he wanted. Not in the way *she* obviously wanted. There was no point in torturing himself by letting the hard, pulsing ache he had for her go to waste.

He got to the bar early and sat drinking a beer and chatting with the bartender. The beer was soothing on his tongue, and the conversation was easy on the brain. He ignored the occasional clench in his belly that told him he wasn't so much anticipating as dreading the arrival of the three women.

This was what he wanted. Kingsley tried to tell himself that with every sip of his beer, his gaze slipping past the bartender to the mirror reflecting his own ambivalence back at him. He looked calm enough, but in the mirror, he saw his fingers tap impatiently on the bar, his lips tighten in disgust when he thought of what would happen with the women upstairs in one of the hotel beds. A date like this would be any other man's ultimate fantasy. But…

He blew out a breath.

Kingsley saw the women coming up to him in the mirror before they spoke.

"We're glad you made it," the curvy one said.

They were all similarly dressed again. Tube dresses in different pastel shades, high heels, hair long and loose around their shoulders. From the look of them, he sensed they would be interchangeable in bed, deliberately so even as they tried to outdo one another in pleasing him. He'd been there before. Suddenly he made a decision.

"I actually came to tell you in person that I can't stay."

He internally winced as their faces fell as one. "Something else came up, and I didn't want to be rude," he said.

The one who'd approached him first looked the most disappointed. She came close and dropped a hand on his thigh, blue fingernails sinking into the thin denim of his jeans. "Are you sure? We have plenty to drink, and eat, upstairs."

The one who reminded him of Adah, lush-hipped and a mouth that hid its own smiles, wrapped her arm around her friend's middle and pulled her back. "We're disappointed, but we also understand—right, Katya?"

The third one nodded and looped her arm through the first girl's. "You're missing out," she told Kingsley as she licked her full bottom lip and tipped her shoulders back to emphasize her breasts.

He tried to look regretful. "As tempting as you all are, I can't. There's something else I need to do tonight."

That *something* turned out to be standing in his kitchen and drinking another beer. Hours later, he stood looking out his kitchen window and wondering what Adah was doing at that exact moment. If she burned like he did. He pressed the beer bottle to the center of his bare chest and sighed at the coolness of it, imagined that it was the touch of her lips on his skin. He hissed in reaction when the bottle brushed across his nipple.

No. He wasn't doing this right now.

But his hardness pushed against the front of his jeans, demanding relief. He gripped the beer bottle in his fist instead and rested it on the counter. His sex throbbing, Kingsley stared out into the dark evening and wished he was a less honorable man.

Kingsley stretched out on the beach, a thick blanket separating his skin from the fine-grained sand while sunglasses covered his eyes and the sun warmed him through a glistening layer of sunscreen. He wasn't scheduled to compete today. It was just a day for him to take it all in.

He pillowed his head on his backpack and watched the dozens of windsurfers race across the water, their multicolored sails whipping against the background of the deep blue sky.

Desperately needing the escape, he'd climbed out of his tangled sheets to watch the day's competition. He couldn't stop thinking about Adah. He'd dreamed of her—their limbs entwined, bodies joined, satisfaction exploding between them. Hours later, he still burned.

"Hey, why aren't you up there?" Max wandered down the beach toward him, his board shorts and T-shirt flapping in the breeze. He pointed to a place farther out from the competition arena where kiters were just enjoying the air and showing off for one another.

"Not feeling it today." Even as he said it, Kingsley winced. He *always* felt like kiting; damn near everyone knew that. That was why he was on the island in the first place. But thoughts of Adah were keeping him earthbound.

There was something irresistible about her, even after finding out about her impending marriage. It was a cliché straight out of one of his sister's novels. Kingsley had been into other women before, but never like this. Maybe his obsession was so intense because he'd never gotten her into bed. Maybe.

He sighed. "I'm a little sore from being on the water all day yesterday," Kingsley told Max truthfully enough. "I need a break."

Although Max hadn't known Kingsley long, Kingsley could sense the other man didn't believe him.

"What's her name?" Max laughed. "Is it one of the girls from yesterday?"

Something in Kingsley's face must have told him otherwise because he gave him a knowing look. "Ah, another girl then. Someone from before."

Kingsley didn't bother to lie. Adah was in his blood, throbbing through his veins into the seat of his sex. It wasn't something he could hide.

"It's not going to go anywhere. She's committed to somebody else."

"If she could only see all the girls trying to pull

you on this island," Max said. "She would jump on you in a heartbeat."

"This isn't about scarcity, my man. If she wants me, she can have me. I'm pretty easy, and she knows it. She just doesn't want to take what's right in front of her."

"That's not something anybody here will believe," Max said. "She has to be crazy not to just snatch you up. Even I can say objectively you're not bad-looking for a guy."

"Thanks." Kingsley had to laugh.

"Anytime, buddy." Max slapped Kingsley on the shoulder and stood up, brushing the sand from his knees. "I'll see you later. This breeze is too nice to waste."

"Yeah, later." The breeze really *was* nice, its strong gusts coming from the direction of Venezuela and bringing with it the faint scent of flowers and fresh coconuts.

Any other day and Kingsley would've been in the air even though he wasn't scheduled for any events; he loved the sport that much. But today he was too distracted.

Everything reminded him of Adah.

He watched Max launch into the air and wondered if his friend could see everything happening on the beach, and if he could see Adah.

Damn. Maybe she was somewhere nearby right now but he just couldn't see her, a problem he wouldn't have if he was in his kite. Kingsley sat up and started to grab his stuff. If he left now, he could be in the air in less than half an hour…

A pair of bare legs and a plastic bag carrying a green coconut appeared in his view.

"Hey," Adah said.

His mood switched so quickly from desperation to relief that he almost felt light-headed.

Cool it, man.

He forced himself to relax, to switch back on the casual flirtation they'd both grown used to. Kingsley deliberately trailed his eyes along her legs, taking his slow and good time appreciating the sheen of her skin, the long limbs he'd imagined wrapped around him, the loose fit of her denim shorts hiding the warm heat he longed to bury his face into. He forced his gaze abruptly higher. That tactic wasn't a good one either.

"What brings you out here?" Kingsley asked. "Are you looking for a new guy to cheat on your old man with?" He clenched his teeth. That was completely uncalled for, but dammit, she had him twisted up in so many knots he didn't know if he was coming or going.

Adah winced at his words and looked ready to bolt. He reached out and grabbed her ankle, startled at how delicate and soft her bones felt between his fingers.

"Sorry." He deliberately bit his tongue. "That was a stupid and mean thing to say. Take a load off. I promise not to say any more dumb things to you. At least not for the next few minutes."

Adah hovered above him, obviously undecided, obviously hurt. He brushed his thumb over her ankle.

"I was being an idiot. It's a bad habit I default to sometimes." Without waiting for her to say yes, he moved to make room for her on his blanket. "Sit. Please."

When she sank gracefully down on the blanket next to him he released the breath he'd been holding. She chewed on the corner of her lip, waiting, it seemed, for him to say something else that would hurt.

"When I don't get what I want, I can be an ass," he said.

"No kidding."

She stayed next to him instead of getting up and walking away like any sane person would. She cradled the plastic bag in her lap, her fingers tugging nervously at the handles of the bag. Then she took out a straw and put it in the coconut, which sloshed with sweet water. She began to drink, watching him from beneath her lashes. Suspicious. Curious.

"Do you want to start over?" she asked.

Christ, yes. He chuckled, shaking his head ruefully. "Her Majesty is so very generous to her foolish subject."

"I learn from the best."

She drank, thirsty and purposeful, from the coconut in her hands and watched him in a way that made *him* thirsty and purposeful. He looked away from her mouth around the straw, to the water and the beach. It was already full of spectators and sun worshippers at half past two in the afternoon. Down the beach, he noticed a familiar trio. The girls from the day before.

They wore bikinis again today, solid-colored bottoms in bright shades with halter tops fringed like western wear. He knew that was the current style now, fringes along bikini tops to make women's breasts look bigger. It wasn't an illusion he appreciated.

His gaze landed on them for only a moment. But it was long enough for them to notice his attention and for all three to notice Adah, who sat like a queen on his blanket, mistress of everything near her, especially him. One of the girls winked at him, and Kingsley raised his eyebrow at her before looking away. He still wasn't interested in what they had to offer.

The sun was hot on his nearly naked body, burning through the white Speedo he'd absentmindedly pulled from the dresser drawer, his mind already on what the day would bring. But with Adah so close and doing a terrible job of hiding her interest in seeing him half-naked, he felt himself stir. Kingsley shifted and cleared his throat, amused. He hadn't lacked this much control of his body since he was a kid and waking up sticky from dreams he barely understood.

"Do you want to go for a drink?" It was early

enough in the day that an invitation like that was a little questionable. But he didn't want to go kiting now, and he certainly didn't want to go swimming with her and expose himself as the desperately horny teenage boy he'd suddenly become.

Adah hesitated a moment before she shrugged. "Sure. I could use something more interesting than this coconut water."

From the sounds she was making with the straw, the coconut water was almost finished. Perfect timing. Without looking, Kingsley reached behind him and into his bag for the jean shorts and T-shirt he'd shrugged off earlier.

"I know the perfect place."

As he pulled on his clothes, he thought about the girls from the day before and the offer they'd made him. A drink and sex. A bar and a bed. Kingsley tried to convince himself he wasn't offering Adah the same thing now.

He finished buttoning his shorts. "You ready?"

"Yeah."

He wanted to feel more regret about leaving the tournament and the beautiful kiting day behind. The wind was perfect and could easily take him high above any sharks or temptations lying in wait for him. But Adah was what he wanted now, her warm presence by his side, her skin that smelled like a sweet-and-spicy mix of ginger and sugar and glowing with more color than when he'd met her. She walked, steady and unafraid, by his side. As if even though she didn't know exactly where Kingsley was going, she would confidently go there with him.

"Have you been in the water today?" he asked.

"Not yet. I was hoping for later this afternoon when the heat is less intense. The water feels really good on my skin near the end of the day."

He hummed a response, mentally tripping over the image of her in the water. Bikini and sunlight. Wet skin and vulnerable belly begging for his touch.

"Sounds like a good way to spend the hottest part of the day." He convinced himself he was being generous for a moment before he opened his mouth again. "You can come over and take a dip in my pool if the sea gets too rough for you, or you don't feel like getting sand in your bathing suit."

She grinned at him, genuinely amused it seemed. "You're so kind."

"I am. I'm glad you finally realized that."

They walked down the beach toward the quieter stretches of sand, past million-dollar houses and empty plots of arid land that investors had yet to take advantage of. Kingsley had thought a time or two about investing in more than just the small house he'd bought for his own private use while he was on the island. Maybe a hotel or restaurant, something separate from his family's corporation and financial interests. But something in him was reluctant to make money from a place he found so much pleasure in. Some deeply buried hippie part of him wanted to keep it "pure" in a way the business part of him thought was highly impractical.

He stopped Adah with fingers on her lower back when they got to the modest beach bar owned by an old friend. "This is us."

She looked over the bar fronting the smooth stretch of white sand and calm water, the quaint wooden structure with a thatched roof and hand-made wooden stools in front. Reggae music played from behind it. On the sand closer to the beach, a half dozen hammocks swayed under the *palapas*, whose coconut-thatched roofs rustled in the perpetual Aruban wind.

A place like this, affordable and old-fashioned in the best way, would normally be overrun by tourists, Kingsley knew. But Josue kept word of it quiet, inviting only a select few to his bar. He didn't turn away the tourists who found him, but he wasn't exactly welcoming to them either. His scowl and crappy service were usually enough to send them packing—even with his delicious rum punch in their bellies—never to return.

"I like this music," Adah said. She was smiling and walking up ahead of him to approach the nameless bar.

From behind the counter, Josue waved at Kingsley. His tersely offered "Afternoon to you" made Kingsley grin.

Josue's broad body moved with slow skill as he mixed drinks for the people taking up space on four of his eight stools. He was by no means the fastest bartender out there, his nearly three-hundred-pound frame with its massive hands weren't made for speed. But everything he concocted was good in a way that made Kingsley do a double take, wondering if he'd been drinking his mai tais and Long Island iced teas wrong all these years. Josue was also a good man. Slow to anger. Steady in his friendships. A solid foundation to the community Kingsley had found on the island. Josue slid tall glasses of a red-and-white drink in front of two of his patrons.

"It's not a *good* afternoon?" Kingsley asked.

"Too early to tell," Josue said, although it was nearly three. He watched Adah approach, sizing her up not unkindly. "Who is this poor thing unlucky enough to meet up with you?"

Kingsley leaned against the bar to exchange a quick hug with Josue before inviting Adah to sit on a stool. Once she sat, he did the same. He introduced them.

"Pleased to meet you, miss," Josue said. "Although you hanging out with this guy makes me worry for you."

"Hey now. I only have the most honorable intentions here."

Josue wiped down the bar, swiping his rag past Adah's resting hands, close enough to give them a pat of sympathy. "What can I get for you?"

Kingsley asked for the rum punch and encouraged Adah to do the same. Ordering the drinks he did in the lounges in Miami seemed a shame and a waste of Josue's considerable skill, although the bartender could make something as simple as a Cuba Libre taste incredible.

"I think I'm in love," Adah said with a wide smile at the bartender once she'd tasted her drink.

"I'll just add you to my list," Josue said, deadpan.

She laughed. After a few minutes catching up with Kingsley, Josue excused himself to tend to the other patrons. The space between them and where Kingsley and Adah sat was enough to give an illusion of privacy. The sound of the waves was a muffling sort of white noise that amplified the effect.

"I'm glad you came out this afternoon," Kingsley told Adah as he turned on his stool to face her. "Although I'm sorry for taking you away from the tournament. The kiters are fun to watch."

Her bottom lip slid from between her teeth, reddened and plush. "To be honest, I only came by to see you."

Her confession wasn't exactly a surprise. But the blood still thudded through his veins when she actually said the words. "You came by to see what your new *friend* was doing?"

"Yes?" The way she made her response a question made Kingsley smile. "The dogs scattered my mind yesterday," Adah continued. "I didn't tell you everything I came to. I thought if I dropped by today in a clearer state of mind, then I could let you know what was going on and really give you an explanation for what happened the other night."

Kingsley wondered if it was just the presence of the dogs that had scattered her mind. If she'd been feeling anything close to what he'd felt, aroused from their proximity to each other and aware of the bedroom not very far away, he understood why her thoughts hadn't been very coherent. It had taken nearly an hour after she left for him to calm down enough to make any sort of sense of the reports he was looking at.

"You want to tell me now?" He wrapped a hand around the thick glass of rum punch. The condensation and coolness seeped into his palm.

"Will you listen?"

"Of course." *I'll listen to anything you have to say all day and all night long.*

She blinked at him, and for a moment, Kingsley thought she'd read his mind. She took a sip from her drink, then looked down the bar to where Josue talked with someone who looked like a relative, only with long hair around his shoulders and a naked back covered in tribal tattoos.

She shook her head, a dismissive motion he was sure would lead to more avoidance on her part. He wasn't wrong.

"This is the life," she said as if she hadn't just asked him to listen to something important she had to say. "Drinking rum punch and sitting at the bar next to a gorgeous man." Kingsley grinned at that, his ego decisively stroked by her casual compliment. "I could get used to this. But I always overthink things. That's my problem."

"There's absolutely nothing wrong with enjoying a warm body by your side and a delicious drink in your belly. That is some of the best stuff of life."

"But I'm sure that's not all you want to do with your life," she said.

"You either," Kingsley responded. "I am very sure of that."

"How can you be so certain when you just met me a couple of days ago? You don't know."

"Well, I do know. You don't strike me as the lazy type."

"I love kids." Adah brushed her thumb against the rim of her glass, a slow back-and-forth motion that distracted Kingsley more than it should have. "Although I don't think I'll have a lot of them, maybe one, maybe none at all after this mess with my engagement, I'd love to be surrounded by them. They're so sweet and innocent, they are the best of us, distilled into the smallest packages."

Kingsley agreed. Someday he, too, would like to have kids, but only after he found the right woman. His gaze lingered on Adah's face, on the beauty and kindness he found there. Someone like her should have children if she wanted them. It was easy to imagine her surrounded by a nest of pillows and propped up in bed with a baby at her breast. He ignored the part of him that thought it should be *his* baby.

He took a quick drink of the punch to moisten his suddenly dry throat. "What makes you think you might not have any children?"

Kingsley watched her stutter over the beginning of a thought. She fidgeted on the stool and did not meet his eyes, her hand moving toward her glass of rum punch, then away without picking it up. He finished his drink with a deep gulp and signaled Josue for another. After his drink came, Josue nodded at him before wandering away again.

"When I was twenty," Adah finally said, "I made a decision I regret now."

An abortion? Kingsley drew a quiet breath of sympathy. He imagined Adah young and studious, a vulnerable girl who'd fallen prey to some slick college senior with pretty words in his mouth to talk her into things she wasn't ready for. A need rose up in him to protect and shelter her.

"Choices are there to be made," he said. "We all have had to deal with difficult ones at one time or another."

Adah glanced down to the other end of the bar again, as if checking to see if anyone was paying any attention to their conversation. But Kingsley knew from experience, as both talker and listener, that people tended to ignore the discussions of foreigners. If Adah had been a local, her business would've been all over the island before she could climb off the stool and head back home. Even Kingsley, someone who came to Aruba every year and made connections with people he found interesting, was generally ignored. Just like he ignored the threads of gossip about some islanders.

"It was stupid," Adah finally said. "My parents were in trouble."

Kingsley's head jerked up. *Her parents?*

"Wait. You didn't have an abortion?"

Adah stopped and wrinkled her brow at him. "What would make you think that?"

He shook his head, gave a soft laugh. "Never mind. Nothing. I was just presuming." Would Adah have allowed herself to be taken advantage of by some ignorant college punk? When she kept frowning, he waved his drink at her in dismissal. "No, really. Keep talking. What you have to say is much better than what I thought you were going to say anyway."

"Okay…" She sucked at the corner of her mouth. "You're a weird guy—anyone ever tell you that?"

"Strangely enough, you're the first."

"People have been lying to you all your life then," she said. "Anyway." She paused again. "My parents have a company they started just after they married. They became partners in life just about the same time they became partners in business. Their company did well for a long time. At least well by their standards. A small niche market loved Palmer-Mitchell Naturals, and they were happy with them as customers." A proud smile lit up her face. "They loved their company."

Kingsley's eyebrows twitched up. He was surprised to hear the name of a company that his sister Adisa loved. She'd never had any chemicals in her hair and swore by everything from the Palmer-Mitchell Naturals line, never abandoning them to get on the bandwagon and embrace other, more popular products that had come along to take advantage of the natural hair care movement.

"But they ran into some trouble along the way, nothing immediate, but it was something they had to deal with using a long-term plan." Adah sounded like she was repeating what had been told to her about the company, not what she had discovered for herself. "They had to find a partnering company to help pull them into a new and more profitable era, especially since the competition has grown exponentially over the years with so many companies that had been in the hair-perming business suddenly creating products for natural hair. They had to create a strategy that would keep them in business and maximize their profits without compromising quality." She paused and looked into the middle distance, a wrinkle forming between her brows as she turned over whatever it was that only she could see.

"My parents brought up a hypothetical situation that involved joining two companies. Theirs with another that would make both stronger. But they wanted to keep the business in the family. Daddy insisted on it and Mother thought it only made sense, especially since she knew of two companies that had gone through the same thing. A business marriage had joined and saved them both."

Kingsley could see where this was going from a mile off. His parents probably would've had the same idea, but he doubted they would have compromised the happiness of any of their thirteen children to make it happen.

"I was in college at the time," Adah said. "I had broken up with a boyfriend and was actually a little burned-out on relationships."

"At twenty years old?" Kingsley remembered what he'd known about relationships as a college student. Precisely nothing. He had only been playing at being a grown-up then.

Adah took a sip of her now-watery rum punch. "In hindsight, it was a foolish promise to make. But I did make it. When my mother asked me to, I offered myself up as half of the company to be joined in marriage to a potential business partner. At the time, it made sense since…" She pressed her lips together, suppressing whatever it was she was about to say. "Anyway, it's done."

"And now you're having second thoughts?"

"Now I'm thinking I made a mistake. Bennett is a great guy—" Kingsley frowned at the mention of another man, her fiancé apparently, feeling an unfamiliar kick of jealousy in his belly "—but he's not the man for me."

"Is he forcing you to go through with the marriage?"

"No. He's been nothing but supportive. He says that whatever I want to do is fine with him. But…" She pressed her lips together again. "This isn't just about me. My parents need this. And I'm the only child they have left."

Kingsley wasn't a believer in no-win situations. Adah was an adult. She was a person who could determine her own future—she didn't have to rely on others to sketch out what that future would look like, especially since she wanted children and was willing to compromise that most basic and essential of desires just to make other people's lives more tolerable. As a businessman and as a person who determined the fate of dozens of people and billions of dollars on a weekly basis, he was already turning over the problem in his head and trying to find a solution.

"You don't have to accept that as the final decision, Adah. You deserve to be happy."

"I know," Adah said, but she didn't sound convinced. "It's been more difficult than ever the last few weeks. The closer we come to finalizing the engagement, the more uncertain I get. I just don't want to let my parents down."

But I don't want you to marry another man. "I know what it's like to have the weight of your family's expectations pressing you down," he said. "It's a burden, and it's also a responsibility. Family, blood and chosen, is important in a way that nothing else will ever be. I understand not wanting to disappoint them." He flexed his fingers around his nearly empty glass. "Ultimately, you have to do what feels right for you."

A sad smile curved Adah's mouth. "I just want to run away from it all."

Kingsley would happily provide that escape for her if that was what she wanted.

"So, now you know my story." She took a long and loud breath.

"I do." Her situation was one he understood too well even though he had happily and gratefully taken over the responsibility of being CEO of his family's company. He had the mind for it, the time and the interest. Unlike most of his siblings, who had other interests and would rather build their fortunes and their financial lives separate from the Diallo empire. "Thank you for sharing it with me."

"You're welcome. And now I think I'm done talking about it." She looked pained, and Kingsley felt like an ass for being the reason she had to dive back into that place that brought her so much discomfort.

Talking about her troubles with a virtual stranger, even if it was someone she wanted to take to bed, obviously only made the pain of it all more intense and amplified the weight of the burden she was trying to avoid. But escape was only a temporary solution. Kingsley's own yearly diversion was temporary, as well. He had no desire to completely sever the responsibilities of being a Diallo. Distance was what he craved, that and the ability to just be himself for a few weeks, separate from the face of the Diallo Corporation, and even from Miami.

"All right," Kingsley said. "Let's be done then." He drained the last of his punch, noticed Adah was nearly finished with hers and ordered another round for them both after she nodded in agreement.

Then another round of drinks and another hour of conversation passed. Kingsley was just telling Adah about his best friend, Victor, and his new wife when he noticed they were about to have company.

A trio of men walked toward them from down the beach, their focused gazes making it clear they were heading for the bar. There weren't enough seats to fit them all.

"Let's move to the beach," Kingsley said to Adah once they'd gotten their latest round of fresh drinks from an amused Josue. She tipped her shoulder in agreement and picked up her drink to follow him across the hot sand.

The water was calm, a nice change from the day he'd arrived. A storm had followed him from Miami to cloud the waters, making the swimming unpleasantly rough for at least two days. The day he'd met Adah was actually the first clear day since he'd been on the island. He'd celebrated that beautiful bit of happenstance with a sunset swim. Tranquil water and Adah. A beautiful and unforgettable correlation. He wished still waters for her as well, so she could see her way out of her dilemma. In the meantime, he'd see for himself what options were available to her.

The *palapa* he led her to was one of seven scattered on the beach in front of Josue's bar. Beyond the bar and farther from the beach was a hotel now closed for renovations. This meant the beach was less busy than usual, nearly empty, the hotel's *palapas* left unoccupied and dozens of unused beach chairs piled nearby. With the bar over a dozen yards behind them and slightly uphill, the stretch of beach felt deserted.

Kingsley guided Adah to the *palapa* that had a hammock already strung beneath it.

"Climb in," he said.

She looked at him, blinking and clutching the glass of rum punch to her chest. "Where are you going to sit?"

He confessed to himself in that moment that he might have been a little bit tipsy. Tipsy enough that sharing a hammock with Adah seemed like a good thing, a practical thing even, to do. They would be talking. They could rest their drinks on the small shelves within arm's reach at the corners of the *palapa*. These were thoughts that he may not necessarily have had while completely sober. Or maybe he just wouldn't have acted on them.

"I'll lay at the other end," he said. That sounded feasible enough.

Adah must have thought so, too, because she handed him her drink, kicked off her sandals and climbed into the hammock, swinging up into the dark cloth in a way that was by no means graceful but incredibly cute. He coughed out a laugh.

"Are you laughing at me?" she asked once she was settled into the depths of the swaying hammock.

"Well, I *am* laughing."

She shook her head and subsided into the swaying thing, one leg hanging over the side. Kingsley put both their drinks on the shelf near her head, then got in beside her, tucking their hips side by side, being careful to keep his feet away from her face. As he settled in at the opposite end, instead of avoiding *her* feet, he clasped them between his hands and rested them on his chest.

"There's sand on my feet," she said, trying to pull them out of his hands.

"I'm sure there's already sand all over me from before," he said and kept her feet right where they were. He dropped his head back and sighed, breathing in the salty sea air and allowing relaxation to overtake his body. "This is nice."

She shifted against him. "Yeah."

He heard her hum again in agreement and felt her gaze on him, but he kept his eyes shut and enjoyed the vague fuzziness in his brain, a luxury he didn't often indulge in. Although he wasn't on duty as CEO of Diallo Corporation while on the island, he usually kept his intoxication to a minimum, wanting to be ready at a moment's notice if anyone from home urgently needed him. Even in his freest moments, he caught himself thinking of his family and other responsibilities. They were never far from his mind. His phone in its waterproof case was zipped into the pocket of his shorts and set to vibrate so he would feel it ring.

It was a long time before he felt Adah's feet relax against his chest; a slow loosening of fine muscles, then her toes drooping to point toward opposite sides of the hammock. With his eyes still closed, he patted the lean line of her foot. He felt a tremor ripple through her leg before he heard the sound of her drinking from her cup. He popped an eye open.

"What about me?" He reached out his hand and she rolled her eyes at him before stretching to the shelf near her to get his drink. Her fingers were hot when they brushed against his, scorching compared with the cool condensation on the glass.

"Thank you." Kingsley lifted his head to drink deeply. He finished it in a few long gulps, then passed the empty glass back to her, the hammock rocking with his movement. Adah's body was so beautifully warm against him, pressed hip to hip, thigh to torso. They lay together in the swaying hammock with the wind buffeting their bodies, the light moving slowly across the sky and the beach toward sunset. It was fast becoming one of the best times he'd ever spent at Josue's bar.

"I feel like I should be doing something else," Adah said, her voice low and relaxed, beautiful to hear after the tension that had vibrated through it while they'd talked at the bar.

"What else do you have to do?" Kingsley asked, trailing his fingers over the tops of her feet. "You're on vacation, aren't you?"

"Like you said, I'm escaping from a situation I've put myself in. I should be strategizing, planning. Or at least planning my outfit for the funeral pyre."

He rolled his head to look at her, very much enjoying the outfit she was wearing now. The shorts showed off her slender thighs and hips while the tank top draped loosely in alluring lines over her modest breasts and flat stomach. "Make sure it's something that catches fire quickly and looks good on Instagram."

She giggled. "What do you know about Instagram?"

"I have younger brothers and sisters I need to keep an eye on. I know every way there is for them to get into trouble."

"Damn. Really? You sound like a scary big brother to have."

"I'm the kind of big brother those hoodlums deserve," he said, feeling the smile spread across his face at the thought of his younger siblings. All of them, even the two who were married and living lives beyond the house where they'd all grown up in Miami.

Adah caught the smile and turned away to put her drink on the shelf nearby, something unreadable on her face. When she turned back to him, Kingsley saw envy, admiration.

"Do you have any siblings?" he asked.

The look on her face changed, became one of pain. "No. Not anymore."

Damn. "You don't have to talk about it if you don't want to."

She fumbled for her glass and took a long swallow from it, draining it down to half. "Good, then I won't." She put the drink back and her head lolled in the hammock as she looked at him, then away toward the horizon where the sun was beginning to spread the warm colors of sunset. After a moment's quiet, she looked back at him. "Am I a downer or what? Pretty soon I won't have anything we can talk about without me crying my eyes out."

"I haven't seen any tears today. You must be talking about another Adah." He caressed the tops of her feet again, wishing he could take all her sorrow away. When she allowed herself joy, she lit up like the sky at noon.

A shaky smile claimed her mouth. "You're surprisingly sweet."

"I'd prefer another adjective, but I'll work with that for now." She bit the corner of her lip, obviously still uncomfortable about where their conversation had meandered before. Kingsley brushed his fingertips along the softness of her toes, her ankles, the bottoms of her feet.

"Oh my God, stop!" She jerked against him,

laughter gushing from her mouth as she yanked her feet away from his hands. With her feet safely out of his reach, her laughter trailed away. She blinked at him as if he'd just betrayed her.

"I guess you're ticklish then."

"Don't even think about it."

"I won't. Promise."

Although she watched him with suspicion, she slowly brought her feet back to him, her muscles tense in preparation to pull back again.

"I always keep my promises, Adah." He said the words very seriously.

"Okay." She relaxed against him again, and he only held her feet between his palms, thumbs making soothing circles around her ankle bones.

"Now, tell me," he said once she was no longer on the brink of flying away from him in a flap of limbs like some startled exotic bird. "What things have you done since you've been here? If I'm going to distract you with an escape, I need to know what you like."

Her lashes flickered low over her eyes, sleepy-tipsy; then she began to talk.

Adah talked like she wanted to release everything. Her exhaustion, her commitments, the secret desires she'd held for herself and away from everyone who knew her.

"I thought about going skydiving, but what if I died?" Her lush eyebrows went up. "Maybe if I died, I wouldn't have to worry about marrying Bennett."

Kingsley let that comment go without making one

of his own, let her continue what was essentially a monologue on what she loved or thought she loved or wanted to try. He continued to caress her feet, delicate touches of his fingers that soon had her squirming against him while she talked and he responded with hums of agreement or some input on his own experience with that particular thing. He tried to ignore the minute movements of her body alongside his, the hot press of her thigh against his thigh, her hips rocking in a subtle but rhythmic motion that helped move the hammock in the breeze.

It built a slow arousal in him, the sensation of her skin beneath his fingers, her undulations, the purr of her voice entangled with the sound of the sea. The noise from the bar behind them seemed far away, so far away that he could easily pretend it didn't exist.

"I'm not too interested in De Palm Island, but I did try it once," he said in response to one of her comments.

"What did you think?"

"You should try it for yourself, then tell me what *you* think."

She tilted her head to look at him, her tongue caught between her teeth. Kingsley's fingers gripped tighter than they should have. He felt the catch of her breath in the way her feet moved, not a flinch but a twitch that spoke of something else than an awareness of pain.

A bolt of arousal churned Kingsley's hips in the hammock and her gaze dipped to his lap, and stayed.

"I don't think…"

When she didn't say anything else, he let go of her feet, tucked them together near his shoulder. He didn't mistake her look of disappointment for anything else, and it was that more than anything that made him climb from the hammock, making it sway dangerously. She gripped its edges, simply looking up at him, watching to see what else he would do.

Kingsley had nearly four drinks in him. He should leave this alone and go back to his house and handle things with a few strokes of his hand. Instead he climbed back into the hammock so they were facing the same direction, sighing in gratitude and anticipatory pleasure when she slid back to give him room. His hips in the hammock next to hers, then their legs stretching out together, their bellies touching, his head rising up higher than hers to look down into her waiting eyes and see what she would do, wait for what she would say.

"Kingsley…"

The way she said his name undid him. He cupped the back of her neck, moaning quietly at the arousal that pooled in his belly, heavy and warm. He could smell the rum punch on her breath, the lingering remains of some sort of flavored lip balm.

"There's a ride on the island you should try…" He dipped his mouth toward hers the same time that she moaned out a laugh, but it was perfect. *She* was perfect.

Their lips came together in an openmouthed kiss

that was immediately hungry, wet. Her mouth under his was so pulse-poundingly arousing that he cursed himself for not indulging again long before now. It might have been the place, the rush of the ocean over the sand—like a whisper of *yes, yes, yes*—it might have been the way her legs shifted against his as she turned into the shelter of the hammock, or it might have even been the sunset's burn in the sky above them. Whatever it was made him ache with lust and want and desire and everything in between.

Her hand slid up his chest, over his shirt to the bare skin of his throat. She was a yielding, soft thing to his kiss, but the way her hand drifted to his throat spoke of firmer desires. And he remembered all too well the way she'd raked her nails across his chest and nipples the night of Elina's party. He wanted that ferocity from her again. The ache in his groin demanded it.

She must have read his mind because her tongue slid firmly into his mouth, meeting his stroke for stroke, a wet snaking, powerful and fierce, that negated anything that he had ever thought about her being a tender thing to be seduced. She took her pleasure from the kiss just like he did, meeting the demanding caress of his tongue with one of her own, the wet slide of their mouth, the slow curl of her hips against his in the hammock. Their hips rocked together. Slow. Hard.

A dim part of Kingsley, the sober part, wanted to say something, wanted to stop himself, but their kiss was quickly becoming something beyond his control. He tightened his hand at the back of her neck and heard himself actually growl when she licked his mouth, her tongue hot and sweet, so damn good that he felt it all the way down to his toes and every spot in between.

Kingsley cursed. "I want you," he gasped into her mouth. "I want you so damn bad…"

He gripped Adah's hips to keep her still, the most he could do toward self-control, aware in some part of his mind of Josue's bar behind them somewhere in the darkness, the constant flow of customers moving to the bar, then away, tourists walking along the beach at a polite distance from the *palapas*. But Adah still squirmed against him. She rubbed her hard nipples against his chest through the layers of fabric, groaned her pleasure into his mouth.

He felt her hand slide down his chest, aware of every movement of her palm over the thin material of his shirt, nails scratching him through the cotton. His breath sped up, and he pressed even more into their kiss, gripping her tight to him with the spread of his hand at the back of her neck and the other traitorous hand on her hip, guiding her small movements against him. He ripped his mouth from hers, breathing too fast, trying not to embarrass himself in his shorts. But she wouldn't let him go, and he thanked every deity he could think of when she slid her hot palm under his shirt, over the shifting muscles of his back, then down over the rough denim of his shorts, guiding him in the intimate dance they were doing on the public beach.

"We shouldn't do this." Kingsley thought she was the one who spoke. It had to be her because he was beyond speech.

He felt the puff of her breath against his mouth before her tongue licked his teeth and slid against his again. A damp and ecstatic sound gathered lightning at the base of his spine. She *must* have said it. Or maybe he did. But then hands slipped between them. His or hers. And he felt the rough fabric of her jean shorts, the hard disk of her button, then her zipper. She moaned into his mouth, lips sliding away from his in a pant of hot breath against his ear, his jaw. He yanked down the front of her jeans, fumbled at the edge of the soft fabric of her panties and found—

Adah hissed in his ear, bit down on his shoulder, and that was all the incentive Kingsley needed to continue the creep of his fingers past the edge of her panties, over the coils of her pubic hair to the slickness of her waiting for him.

She sobbed into his throat. Her fingernails scraped down his back and clenched into the muscles of his ass through the rough denim shorts.

It felt so *good*. It felt so good they had to stop.

"Adah…we should—"

But she opened her legs, and he was lost. Heart stuttering in his chest as she flung her thigh over his and sank her nails deeper into his flesh. He claimed her mouth again, licking its hot interior the way he wanted to lick the womanly softness of her. She was wet and hot around his fingers, swollen with desire for him. He stroked her slickness, and she moaned.

His tongue flicked out and mirrored the motion of his fingers inside her panties and he could hear her panting through the scant space between their mouths when they pulled back from each other, gasping for breath, their mutual eagerness feeding the other, his fingers moving in her slickness, then up to the firm button of her pleasure. She jerked against him, a frantic motion that pushed the cradle of her hips against his hardness and made him even harder. The want throbbed so fiercely in his shorts that it *hurt*.

He gripped her hips again, this time to press himself even harder against her, the two of them moving in delicious counterpoint to each other, Kingsley high against her hip and Adah against the finger stroking her eager clitoris.

His head swam in the heady scent of their desire and he drank up the sounds she made, sucking her tongue, licking her lips, her teeth, nibbling at her throat, anything he could reach. He'd never tasted anything more tempting. He wanted more.

With a more deliberate and focused motion, Adah bucked against him as her fingers raked his back.

"I'm—"

"—close."

They bucked against each other in the same moment, her flesh tightening around his fingers. That was all it took to yank him over the threshold with her, a gush of heated wetness in his shorts. Dimly he thought he should be embarrassed, but the feel of his spilled desire only made him want to strip off her panties, her shorts, her little shirt, and lick her entire body until he became hard enough again to slide inside her body and take them both toward pleasure once more. He was nearly mindless with it.

Adah pulled her mouth away from Kingsley's and pressed her forehead into his throat. He held on to her, curving his palm protectively around her sex while small twitches and pulses moved her against him. His heart pounded in his chest; his breath huffed out of control. The sun had dipped completely behind the horizon and left the sky painted in violets and gray, clouds trailing across the deep bruise of it.

Slowly, as his breath came back to him, Kingsley rubbed the small of Adah's back while curses and recriminations slowly began to grow from the postorgasmic hush of his mind. Despite the lack of a real commitment to her man, what they'd just done was wrong. He didn't do this kind of thing. Ever. Kingsley licked his lips to speak.

But she beat him to it. "I shouldn't have done that. I'm sorry."

Although he'd wanted it as much as she had—maybe even more—Kingsley had to agree with her. The orgasm helped burn away the last of his alcohol buzz, and the resulting clarity was brutal.

"It's my fault. I shouldn't have let it get this far."

She was as still as death against him. "Me either." Adah apologized again, apparently completely sober, too, and began to climb from the hammock. "I should go."

Although Kingsley thought he was the one who should leave, the filthy state of his shorts stopped him from declaring his own intention. He swayed in the hammock after she climbed from it, feeling cold where her body had pressed so warmly against his before. Even in the dark, he felt the brush of her eyes over his crotch, the hem of his shirt dragged up to his bare chest and the new marks she'd made there.

He cursed again. "I'm sorry." Because he'd been the one to climb into the hammock with her, to kiss her like the right belonged to him.

"I know," she said.

Then she was gone.

Chapter 6

Adah made it back to her hotel on shaking legs. The cab ride there had given her enough time to replay every delicious yet horrible moment of her loss of control with Kingsley. She'd only had three drinks, only three, so it wasn't much of an excuse. Just like the last time she and Kingsley had ended up together. She was weak for him. Inexcusably weak. Well, maybe it had been four drinks.

"Adah, is that you?" Her mother's voice came through the slightly open door between their rooms.

Who else would it be in my hotel room? She thought the words but did not say them out loud. There was no reason to take out the result of her bad judgment on her mother.

"Yes, Mother." She sounded like a kid again, vulnerable and guilty, but she didn't have it in her to disguise her tone.

"Do you want to have dinner soon?" Her mother appeared in the doorway looking like she was on the way to a bridge game with the girls in a pale blue sheath dress and her hair braided in a high Cleopatra crown.

What Adah wanted to do was shower, then crawl into bed and stay there for the rest of her stay in Aruba. But she wasn't going to be a coward.

"That sounds great. Let me just take care of a few things first."

From the doorway, Thandie frowned, her eyes picking apart Adah's expression. "Are you okay, honey?" She started to come closer, bringing with her the powdery scent of her perfume.

But Adah quickly backed away. She wasn't sure she wouldn't collapse under the weight of her mother's concern and simply confess everything. "I'm fine. I just need a couple of minutes." She grabbed her phone off the bedside table and escaped into the bathroom.

With the door firmly closed and at her back, she dialed Bennett's number.

"Hey," she said when he answered. "Can you talk?"

Adah heard a busy hum in the background, the usual chaos whenever she called him. He never seemed to be alone or unoccupied.

"Not right now. But how about in an hour?"

"Okay. That sounds good."

"Cool."

Adah disconnected the call and put the phone on the edge of the sink. She pressed her lips together and stared at her reflection in the mirror. Trembling fingers lifted to touch her bruised-looking lips, the flush she could still feel in her cheeks.

She looked like she'd just climbed from a lover's bed. Hair messy and wild despite the braid she'd pulled it into only hours before. A bruise forming just under her jaw from the press of Kingsley's teeth.

Between her legs was slippery and hot, and without closing her eyes she could still feel Kingsley's touch, firm and insistent, between her thighs. A shivery pleasure undid her. She felt both loose and tight, like he'd sunk into the very being of her, leaving all of her sore and bruised and aching for more. Shame and regret coursed through her. Not because of what she'd done with Kingsley, or at least not completely, but because she wasn't being honest with herself. Not about what she wanted, not about what she would do.

Damn, she was spending a lot of time staring in the mirror after making a series of bad decisions where Kingsley was concerned.

But was it a bad decision?

The question came out of nowhere and caught her off guard.

You wanted to be with him. He's a man you're at-

tracted to and who's attracted to you. You enjoy him
touching you in a way you haven't been in years.

Adah squirmed at the truth of it. She planned to
call Bennett and confess, ask his forgiveness for
something that really had nothing to do with him
and everything to do with her. He probably wouldn't
care much about what she did with another man before they officially bound their lives together. Bennett was practical. And he was no hypocrite.

Adah bit her lip, then turned away from the mirror. Time to wash the mistakes from her skin and get
ready for Bennett's phone call. In the shower, she
scrubbed her body under the near-scalding water,
carefully washing between her legs while she tried
not to think about Kingsley. She was mostly successful.

After her shower, she was sitting on the bed
and about to slip into her sandals when her mother
stepped through the door after a quick knock.

"Are you ready, darling?"

"Sure." Adah sighed, knowing that this wasn't
just going to be dinner. It would be another inter-
rogation. And it would be another disappointment.
She couldn't give her mother the answer she needed,
not yet. Not until she confessed what she'd done to
Bennett and got her conscience clear so she could
start their new life together in a way that made her
feel okay about it all. And there was something that
had been gnawing at her.

"Mother… Mama…" Adah pressed her lips together as words she wasn't sure she was ready for built up in her throat. Thinking about this pending marriage to Bennett over the past few months had brought so many things rushing to the front of her consciousness. Things that she'd gone through years of therapy for but still not managed to release.

"What is it, love?" Thandie stepped closer, concern in her face. Her hands fluttered up to gently press into Adah's cheeks. They both knew it wasn't every day Adah called her "Mama."

There was nothing for her to do but say it. "Do you wish it was me instead of Zoe who died?"

"What are you saying?" Her mother flinched back and her hands dropped away from Adah's face. "Why would I wish something like that?" She drew a trembling breath and took Adah's hands in hers. Her fingers were ice cold. "What's wrong, honey?"

"This marriage and the family business. It just seems like it would all be easier if Zoe was the one dealing with them instead of me. She would've been so much better at all of this."

"No, no! We almost lost both of you. You were in the hospital for so long after the accident…" Sudden tears washed down her mother's cheeks, and Adah felt instantly guilty. More guilt on top of the old. She'd nearly forgotten about her long hospital stay, the weeks she'd missed school. "Your father and I loved Zoe, and we love you, too," her mother said.

"We'd never trade you for her! Never. Don't say that again, please." Her voice broke. "Please."

Once Adah started, though, she couldn't stop. "I feel so guilty sometimes that I was the one who survived and not Zoe—"

"There's nothing for you to feel guilty about! You weren't driving the car that took Zoe away from us. You didn't do anything wrong."

"I can't help what I feel. You want this marriage so badly and I—"

"You don't want to go through with it?" Thandie shook her head quickly, not waiting for Adah to finish. "You don't have to do this if you don't want to. *Any* of it." She squeezed Adah's hands so hard it hurt. "Your father and I have been proud of you all these years. We love you. If you don't want this, all you have to do is say so."

Adah didn't believe for a moment it was that simple. Palmer-Mitchell Naturals needed rescue. Perhaps not at this moment, but definitely sometime in the very near future. If the merger with Leilani's Pearls didn't go through because of Adah, not only would her parents be disappointed; the business they'd nurtured for years would be left in ruins.

"Mama, I don't—"

A knock on her door cut off the rest of her words. She frowned and exchanged a look with her mother, who squeezed her hands once more before releasing them.

"Are you expecting company?" Her tone was soft, but something in Thandie's face said who she thought it might be.

"No." Even though she hadn't known him long, she was sure Kingsley would never show up at her door unannounced. That was her habit of bad behavior, not his. She went to answer the knock, feeling her mother's eyes on her with every step. Frowning, she opened the door.

"Has it been an hour yet?"

Adah stared at Bennett. "Hi!"

"I figure a visit is better than a call. What do you say?"

Bennett Randal stood in the doorway, larger than life and smiling with mischief in his cinnamon-brown eyes. He wore blue suede shoes, slim-fitting jeans and a pale blue dress shirt rolled up at the elbows.

Adah blinked at Bennett, unable to get over her shock at seeing him. He didn't wait for her welcome, or lack thereof. He stepped into the room and greeted Adah's mother.

"It's good to see you, Mrs. Palmer-Mitchell," he said, dropping a kiss on the older woman's jaw and making the mouthful of a last name sound both elegant and easy.

"What a pleasant surprise." Her mother welcomed him with a warm hug. "Adah and I were just about to go out for dinner. Would you care to join us?" A smile as wide as all of Aruba lit up her face.

Bennett glanced over his shoulder at Adah, who could do nothing but stare at him. "Well, if you don't mind, I'd actually like to have some time alone with Adah. It's been a while since she and I saw each other, and I believe we have a lot to discuss."

"Of course, of course." Her mother looked more and more pleased with each passing moment. "I can have room service brought up for myself, or head out to join some new friends who're dining in town tonight." She made a shooing motion, like she was passing Adah off to Bennett.

"Thank you." He kissed her cheek again before making his way to Adah. "Are you ready?"

"Um…yes. Sure. Let me…let me just grab my bag." She still didn't know what to expect from Bennett's surprise visit. The ground was shifting too quickly under her feet.

"Good," Bennett said with his trademark dimpled smile.

After she grabbed her purse, clutching the small leather strap like a lifeline, she fell in step with Bennett, who waited in the middle of the room, completely at ease in his designer jeans and platinum watch, looking curiously around the room. If it had been anyone but Bennett, Adah would've cringed at the untidiness. But Bennett was familiar enough with how she kept her living space, had visited her in college enough times to see the piles of clothes and books stacked on various surfaces, her laundry basket full with weeks' worth of laundry.

If it had been Kingsley, on the other hand… She yanked her mind away from Kingsley. There was only one direction things would go from there, and she wasn't ready to think those thoughts with her mother or Bennett standing right there.

"Let's go," she said to Bennett. "I'm ready."

"Excellent. A buddy of mine told me about this place that's supposed to have real Aruban food. We'll head there and see what the rest of the night holds."

They said good-night to Adah's ecstatic mother and stepped out into the hallway. Away from her mother's probing gaze, Adah drew a steadying breath. "What are you doing here? I thought you were in Monaco or Dubai someplace."

"I was, but I figure I was needed more urgently here. Plus the partying over there gets a little stale after a while."

"I'll take your word for it," Adah said with a reluctant smile.

"Please do."

Despite her feelings on what happened between her and Kingsley, just Bennett's very presence brought her close enough to a good mood. He loved and lived life with such joie de vivre and passion that being around him was like getting a shot of energy.

She didn't know where he found the stamina to be all over the world, all over Atlanta, party until

dawn, then perform his duties as chief strategy officer for his family's company. His job was luckily
one he could perform remotely, and he did it well if
current profitability statistics that her parents rou-
tinely shared were anything to go by.

Naturally, Bennett had rented a car when he got
to the island. He guided Adah to a white compact
car in the hotel's parking lot and opened the door for
her, waited until she was properly settled in the passenger seat before firmly closing the door. He sank
into the driver's seat and started the engine.

"So how are things going with my wayward fian-
cée?" He skillfully guided the car out of the nearly
full parking lot and onto the road like he knew where
he was going. Maybe he did; maybe he was as familiar with the island as Kingsley was.

Adah ducked her head, wincing at the thought of
the man she apparently couldn't get out of her mind
for five damn seconds. "Don't even joke about that."

"That bad, huh?"

She sighed and fiddled with her seat belt, ready
to tell him everything, or at least the edited version
of what had happened between her and Kingsley on
the beach. "I can't go through with the wedding."
She blinked. That was *not* what she'd planned to say.

"Okay," Bennett said.

She felt his eyes on her, a comforting sensation

despite her own dawning horror of what just came out of her mouth. "That's all you're going to tell me?"

"Do you want me to say more?" Bennett tilted a playful brow her way. "No one is going to force you to marry me, Adah. I've seen you struggle with this decision practically since the day you made it. The only person dragging you kicking and screaming to the altar is you."

"Don't say that!"

He chuckled. It wasn't a mean sound, but it did make her feel a little foolish. "Having our families joined by this damn agreement would be great for the company and for the idea that our parents had, and the key word here is *had*. But we adapt and change to circumstances, my girl. And this, you falling for some surfer in the middle of nowhere—"

"He's not a surfer!" She sputtered despite herself.

"Definitely qualifies as a change in circumstances," Bennett finished.

Adah pressed her palms against her face and shook her head. She was still wrestling with the words that had jumped out of her mouth without permission. Was she willing to commit to them and call off the wedding based on nothing but a couple of heavy petting sessions and eleventh-hour jitters?

"I just can't do this," she said again. "I…he and I hung out today and things went further than I planned."

Bennett took his gaze from the road to glance at her in surprise. "You finally got some?"

Her face flushed. "Oh my God, stop! You're just as bad as Selene."

Another smile, something warmer, almost indulgent, flickered across his mouth. "There are worse comparisons you could make."

He was right about that. Selene was one of the best women, the best *people*, she knew in the world. Adah remembered telling her friend about the plan to marry Bennett and save Palmer-Mitchell Naturals. Selene had asked her if she was sure, talked her through the cons of her decision and later comforted her when the doubts struck.

Selene never thought the decision was the right one, but when Adah, in a fit of annoyance, had snapped at her to drop the subject, Selene let it go and never brought up her reservations again. And even as the years went by and Adah began to voice her own doubts, not once had Selene said "I told you so." Adah didn't think that, in the reversed position, she would have been that noble. She sighed.

"So what's up with you and this guy anyway?" Bennett asked. "Are you two trying to elope or something?" He skillfully guided the car through the narrow streets, one hand on the wheel while he changed gears with the other, occasionally glancing away from the road to rest his gaze on her face. "I hope you're not basing a life decision on the ability of one guy to rock your world."

"Please! I'm not that impulsive." *Almost, but not quite.*

"Just making sure, love. You know I have no problem with you changing your mind about this marriage thing. Our parents will get over it and make other plans, but I don't want you to get hurt. Not even by your own decisions."

Adah tucked her tongue between her lips, thinking very carefully before she spoke. "It's not about him—I mean, yes, I met him and he…affected me in ways I never expected, but I've been indecisive for a while now. You know that."

"I do. I do." He pulled the car into the parking lot of a one-story colonial building, the gravel crunching under the tires. "As long as you do, too. Men are interesting creatures." He looked at her as he turned off the engine. "And by interesting, I mean we think with our dicks most times. And we assume women think with their hearts and make decisions based on their lust for marriage, or whatever. If he knows the whole story, he might think you're breaking this thing off just for him. That might scare him off."

Adah shook her head. "I don't think that'll happen. I've been pretty clear that, I'm…" What exactly was she doing anyway?

"Just having fun in Aruba and he could've been any guy as far as your sweet little libido is concerned?"

She laughed, even while heat flooded her cheeks. Bennett had always been able to make her blush and laugh easily. "Not exactly. But it's been really physical between us, and I want to explore that without feeling guilty about hurting you." Although they both knew Bennett wouldn't be hurt by anything she did. She wondered if he even had a jealous bone in his body. He applied his own "live and let live" attitude to everybody around him.

He gave her a look that said exactly that. "Watch out for your own tender bits, little one."

Adah shook her head, smiling so widely that her cheeks hurt. How could she have thought marriage would work between her and someone who called her these ridiculous names? *Little one.* She loved him for that and for his overall tenderness, and for never pretending the feelings between them were something different from what they were.

"I love you, Bennett."

He helped her out of the car with a grin. "Don't let your mother hear you say that. She'll get the wrong idea."

At the mention of her mother, Adah rolled her eyes and dared to make a joke. "It's not her fault you're perfect son-in-law material."

They walked into the restaurant together, a homey space with paintings of different landmarks around Aruba hung on the walls, glass display cases containing small pieces of handmade local jewelry for sale, and tables spread out at a comfortable distance from one another.

The host immediately greeted and seated them

and had barely turned to go back to his post when a waiter came with water and an offer to get them something stronger. The waiter took their orders and quickly left, the height of efficiency and good customer service.

"Mama's going to kill me when she finds out I called off our engagement," Adah said once they were alone again.

Bennett laughed at her. "You'll survive this, and so will she."

"And the family business?"

"It'll be fine, too."

Since the marriage agreement had been made, Leilani's Pearls, thanks to Bennett's hard work and business sense, had recovered to the point where they didn't really need Adah's parents anymore. Any decision Adah made now would affect her family more so than Bennett's.

Adah cursed. "I feel so selfish right now."

"It's not selfish to want to be happy, doll."

"Of course you'd say that."

"It doesn't make it any less true." He tapped the back of her hand with two fingers, his version of reassurance. "Life is too damn short to make sacrifices this big."

Across the table from her, he looked relaxed and happy, a man without a care in the world. Would he be sacrificing anything if their marriage went on as planned?

"What about you, Bennett? Isn't there anyone who makes you reconsider any of this?"

He drew his hand back and braced his forearms against the table. The handsome planes of his face went blank as he seemed to think about his answer. "There's someone I would give this all up for if she was interested in me the way I'm interested in her," he finally said. "But she isn't, so my feelings don't matter."

Adah drew back, surprise blowing into her chest like a sonic boom. She'd asked the question almost as a hypothetical, believing that someone like Bennett simply lived and loved because he wanted to, not in reaction to the fact that a woman didn't want him the way he wanted her. "I'm so sorry," she said softly.

"Don't feel sorry for me, doll face. I got over that a long time ago."

She didn't believe him. "Okay…"

The waiter came then to bring their drinks and took orders for their meals. Bennett took a slow sip of his wine and gave Adah a pained look. "I didn't come here to talk about me," he said.

"And I didn't come to Aruba to fall into bed with a well-hung stranger either."

Bennett cringed the same time Adah did. "That was *way* too much information."

"I know, right?" She pressed fingers to her lips, embarrassed and shocked at herself. "I don't even know—" But she cut herself off before anything else could come out of her mouth. Bennett was already looking at her in disbelief.

"So you haven't even slept with this stud yet?"

"Sort of. I mean, we…" She blushed as she said the words, unable to continue.

"Again, even though I just asked, let's just keep it to broad strokes, shall we?"

A giggle bubbled up from Adah's throat. "So to speak."

"An unfortunate choice of words." He grimaced like he'd just found out where babies actually came from, and she nearly doubled over in laughter, reaching for his hand across the table and holding fast, so grateful for him and the way he was able to help her forget about her problems.

"I'm so glad you came tonight."

He smiled back and squeezed her hand. "Good. I figured face-to-face was the best way to have this conversation. That way you couldn't bullshit your way out of what you needed to say."

"I was going to call you and confess all my sins, then agree to set the wedding date."

"My little martyr."

The sound of laughter near the entrance of the restaurant drew Adah's gaze. A blonde head appeared— Annika from the nighttime snorkeling trip. She had her hands in the pockets of a stylish jumpsuit that skimmed her model-lean figure. Still laughing, she turned her head to look at someone walking up behind her. A blond man Adah didn't recognize. Then

Kingsley walked in, gorgeous in a white, open-necked shirt and dark jeans. Adah lost her breath.

Although he seemed completely engaged in the conversation with Annika, he looked around the restaurant as he walked in and immediately saw Adah. His eyes narrowed, and the animated look on his face become more subdued.

She snatched her hand from Bennett's. With a complete lack of tact, he turned to look toward the source of the noise and took in what was going on with a quick sweep of his gaze.

"That's your new friend?" But it was more of a statement than a question. "We should go say hello." His dimples flashed with mischief.

Adah frantically shook her head.

"No. We shouldn't." But telling Bennett what to do was like telling lightning not to strike. He gave Kingsley an appraising look, watched him and his party get seated on the opposite side of the small restaurant. Just as Bennett was about to get up and make a nuisance of himself, their food arrived. Adah breathed a soft sigh of relief.

But she had no sooner picked up her fork to eat when a quiet presence moving across the restaurant and toward their table drew her attention. She looked up with the fork clenched in her hand.

"Adah." Kingsley approached the table with the confident and predatory rock of his hips that made

Adah's mouth water. "I didn't expect to see you again today."

Again. Both she and Bennett would have had to be deaf not to hear the significance of that word.

She cleared her throat. "It's good to see you." She deliberately avoided the word *again*, then swallowed, put her fork down. "I didn't think I'd leave the hotel for the rest of the night, but Bennett paid a surprise visit." She gestured to him sitting across the table from her, and he stood up, holding out his hand to shake.

"I've heard a lot about you," he said to Kingsley, and Adah wanted to kick him.

Kingsley offered his own hand and his first name. "I may have heard a thing or two about you."

Was it her imagination or did he grip Bennett's hand a little too hard?

"Will you be in town long?" Kingsley asked after he released Bennett's hand. He stuffed his hands in the pockets of his slacks, the equivalent, Adah thought, of wiping off his hands.

"Not very." Bennett stayed standing. "I'm making a quick stop over to see this lovely young woman before I head back to the States."

"Well, I hope you enjoy everything the island has to offer while you're here. It's a beautiful place, and not only because Adah is here." He dipped his head once to indicate Adah and to catch her eye.

"I'll keep that in mind," Bennett said, his eyes flashing merciless amusement at Adah's expense.

A hiccup of awkward silence made Adah want to say something, but she held her tongue before something stupid could trip off of it. More seconds of stilted silence ticked by while the two men loomed over her, looking at each other.

"I'll let you get back to your meal," Kingsley finally said. "It was good to meet you—Brandon, was it?"

Bennett corrected him with a cheerful flash of teeth. "Same here." He sank down into his chair before Kingsley could step away, apparently bored of the game now. "I'm sure I'll see you again."

"I'm not so confident of that. But we'll see what the future holds." He looked at Adah again. "Take care."

She swallowed the hard lump in her throat and could only nod at him before he turned away and headed back to his friends. Adah could hear their voices speaking in Dutch and laughing easily. She didn't watch him walk away. She couldn't.

"Well. He certainly wants a repeat performance."

Adah ducked her head, still unable to speak. Her stomach was twisted up in knots and the food that seemed so appetizing before now made her turn away in revulsion.

"You okay, little one?" Bennett asked, taking her hand.

"Not really."

"Do you want to leave?"

She shook her head, and her entire body trembled

with the violence of the motion. "No. Let's stay. I know you're hungry. I'll get over this."

But it was unbearable. Kingsley's presence had destroyed any sense of equilibrium she'd found after her conversation with Bennett. Nearly an hour later, with her plate mostly full and her stomach still too twisted to do any of the formerly delicious-looking food justice, Adah wished she was anywhere but in the restaurant where she could still hear the sound of Kingsley and his friends' conversation, the rumbling bass of his voice, their laughter that continued uninterrupted.

Bennett put down cash for the meal, his dessert finished.

"Let's go. Any more of this and I feel like I'm torturing you." He didn't wait for her to get up, just pushed his seat back at the same time she gave him a grateful look, her chest still tight with discomfort while her belly churned, a twisted roller coaster. He helped her from her chair and guided her out of the restaurant, apparently trying to be subtle with the placement of his body between her and where Kingsley was sitting.

In the car, he started the engine without comment. When they were back on the road, coasting toward Adah's hotel, she felt his eyes on her again.

"Is there any place you want me to drop you?"

It was such a pointed question that she caught her breath. He wasn't suggesting…? "Wouldn't that be a little presumptuous of me? He might not even go back home after the restaurant."

"He might not. You're right." Bennett tapped his fingers on the steering wheel in thought. "Come out for a drink with me—then I can drop you off at his place later tonight."

Adah wanted to say no. She shouldn't go to Kingsley's and disrupt his life any more than she already had. But the desire to see him was a sudden and demanding ache. Once Bennett suggested it, there was nothing else she wanted more.

"No," she said. "I won't drink tonight, but I will have some ice cream with you." She nearly looked away in embarrassment at Bennett's knowing grin.

"That's my girl." Bennett flashed her a smile and squeezed her shoulder. "Where should I take the fair princess?"

They ended up near Palm Beach and the high-rise hotels. The gelato place Adah chose was the best she'd found on the island so far with enough flavors to satisfy her taste for variety. She insisted on treating Bennett to a second dessert, and they walked through the small shopping area that was alive with browsing tourists and the slow meandering of cars on the small side street.

"Thank you again for this," she said.

Finally, her intense reaction to Kingsley's presence at the restaurant was beginning to subside. The awareness of him was still there, a faint pulse beat under her skin, but it was no longer a fight-or-flight impulse that would only lead to recklessness.

"I couldn't do any less for one of my best girls."

Adah laughed. "I'm not sure what I should say to that."

"How about 'thank you'?"

"Thank you, Bennett." She looped her arm through his, and they walked on.

He kept up an amusing patter of conversation, distracting her with the unusual things he'd done since they'd seen each other last, the people who'd asked him about her in Atlanta, his plans for his family's business and the timeline for implementing them. He was so driven, so skilled that she half regretted his loss from her family. He was the perfect son that her parents had never had.

They meandered back the way they had come, passing the same restaurants again, their gelatos long finished. Despite the street lamps, the darkness felt heavy, rich with possibility. And the significance of that, and the fact that it had nothing to do with Bennett, made her fingers twitch where they rested around her purse strap. Bennett was nothing if not observant.

"You ready to get dropped off?" He showed her the glittering face of his watch. Nearly two hours had passed since they'd left the restaurant.

Adah's fingers tightened on her purse strap. "Sure. Yes." The word wavered in the air, sounding uncertain. Adah tried again. "Yes, I'm ready." This time her voice was stronger. But that still didn't hide how nervous she was.

"We don't have to go right now if you don't want to. There's nothing pressing I need to do either tonight or tomorrow."

God, she loved this man. "Let's walk for a little longer. I can pick up a souvenir for Selene."

"Okay. Let's do it."

But the little time she bought herself getting the aloe skin care set for Selene passed all too quickly. Barely an hour later, she stood on the front step of Kingsley's house while the taillights of Bennett's car retreated into the distance.

She thought of what she would say to Kingsley, how she would explain herself. The memory of another time she'd tried to do the same thing, and how it had failed, came back to haunt her. But there were no dogs chasing her tonight.

Adah rapped her knuckles against the wooden door.

After two rounds of knocking, though, any confidence she had evaporated when Kingsley didn't come to the door. She glanced at his truck parked in the drive, walked back to feel the still-warm hood under the tentative touch of her hand. Adah knocked on the door again, then again. No answer.

Was he spending the night with Annika?

Adah breathed deeply to push away the disappointment and dismay crowding into her throat. She took a step back, ready to call for a cab back to her hotel. Her hand fell to the door handle, and she re-flexively gripped it. A click and the door eased back on quiet hinges.

Startled, Adah stared at the triangle of darkness just inside the door, then walked in without allowing herself to fully think about what she was doing. Timid footsteps drew her into the shadowed living room, its dimensions gradually becoming clear through the moonlight cascading past open blinds, showing her the sparse furniture, the hallway leading to more private rooms.

Softly, she called out Kingsley's name, but there was no reply. Her hands clenched at her sides. She took a step back. Then a step forward, then another until the shadows of the hallway brushed her shoulders, her face. All the doors off the hallway were open.

The first room showed the silent silhouette of a powder room, the other a furnished but otherwise empty bedroom, and the last… Adah drew in a deep and steadying breath.

Kingsley slept naked. His screened windows were open and allowed in the coolness of the night breeze. There were no curtains over them to flap, no blinds to tap distractingly to the rhythm of the fierce wind, no papers to flutter madly about the room. Just Kingsley lying heavily in the bed on top of white sheets, his legs splayed wide, arms above his head, his face turned away from the bedroom door.

Adah truly felt like an intruder. She bit her lip and

took a step back. But the figure in the bed shifted, legs, hips, chest, arms. A full-body movement that dragged her gaze all over him until at last she was looking at his face and his eyes staring at her. Those eyes widened slightly, but other than that, Kingsley gave no sign of being surprised.

"Another unexpected visit, Doe Eyes?" His voice was sleep roughened and dragged along her sensitive nerves, hot and urgent.

She licked her lips. "I wanted to explain about what you saw at the restaurant."

"You don't owe me any sort of explanation." Kingsley scrubbed a hand over his face, grabbed for his cell phone on the bedside table and glanced at its clock before he put it back and gave her his full attention. "You were having a lovely meal with your fiancé. Nothing any woman should have to explain. Especially not to a man she barely knows."

She wanted to tell him not to dismiss his importance to her so easily. She wanted to tell him so many things.

"He's not my fiancé," she settled on saying.

"Fiancé-to-be, then."

"Not even that."

Kingsley sat up in the bed and put his back to the headboard. He drew a deep breath. "What are you saying?" The question sounded weighted, expectant. Or maybe that was just Adah's foolish hope.

"He and I agreed to call off our potential engagement. It wouldn't have worked between us. Bennett is a very good friend. Nothing more."

"From what I've seen, good marriages have been based on less," he said.

Adah didn't want to talk about marriages. She licked her lips, nervous and on the brink of flight. "Do you want me to leave?"

Kingsley's gaze moved down her body, then up, a slow drag full of intent and desire. Then he shifted in the bed again, raising the knee closer to her to shield his lap in a way he hadn't seemed worried about doing before. Instead of replying, he held out his hand.

Adah swallowed. Was this what she wanted? The question seemed foolish enough with the desire pooling like liquid fire in her belly. She was walking across the room to him before she could think anything else. She slid off her sandals and knelt on the bed. His hand closed around hers, warm and firm. He pulled her the rest of the distance across the sheets and against him. With her heart fluttering madly in her chest, she was hyperaware of his nakedness, the press of her clothed body against him, the hot slide of his palm against hers, then his hands along the backs of her hands, up her arms, then higher to clasp just above her elbows.

"I've already told you what I want, Doe Eyes. Now it's your turn."

She shivered at the intensity in his voice, rough

and soft at once, as it rubbed over her sensitive nerves and laid her bare to her own desires.

"I want you," she said. "I've always wanted you."

He didn't seem surprised by her confession. If anything, her words seemed to only confirm what he already knew about the flood of desire that took her over whenever she saw him and thought of him.

"Good," he said. "Now we're finally on the same page."

"And in the same bed."

In the moonlight falling into the room, she saw the corners of his mouth curve up, beautiful and unashamed. No amusement this time, just a predatory certainty.

"Yes," he said. "Finally."

His eyes captured and held hers; then his hand crept to the back of her dress and pulled the zipper down. His fingers traced the line of skin the zipper revealed, a light caress until he reached the end of the zipper at her tailbone and Adah was trembling with need.

"Show me what you want," he said, voice growling, hand on her hip.

She flushed under her open dress while her mind conjured it perfectly. Having him just like this, under her and inside her. Adah crawled over Kingsley, straddled him and pushed him until he lay flat on his back, watching her with his night-dark eyes. He was already hard for her.

Under her flattened palms, his chest rose and fell

with steady, even breaths. She raked her fingers over his muscled pecs, through his chest hair. Even in the dark of night, he was unmistakably gorgeous. A hard and virile man willing to please her.

She slid her parted thighs over his, their flesh brushing with the sound of whispers. "This is what I want," she said.

The long nights in her lonely bed when she did nothing but think of him despite other things looming on her horizon had prepared her for this moment, his skin under hers, the wetness sticking her underwear to her body, him groaning when she settled her bottom on the hard jut of his desire.

"Then take it," he said.

The breath shivered out of her. "Do you…do you have anything?"

Without taking his eyes from her, Kingsley reached back for the drawer of his bedside table, hand fumbling inside until it emerged with a six-pack strip of condoms. He pulled one off and dropped the others on top of the table.

"Just in case," he breathed.

Adah smiled and took the condom from him. "Yeah…?"

He drew in a deep breath when she touched him, his abs tightening, fingers clenching on their tight hold on her hips. He was silk-covered steel in her hand, beautiful and ready for her. With his hardness grasped in her fist, she hovered over him, tugged aside her panties, then slowly lowered herself. Inch by delicious inch.

"Adah…"

She hissed at the stretch of him inside her but didn't stop until she was fully seated on top of him, their pubic hair a delicious and damp tangle. Her dress hung off one shoulder, just a breath away from falling down and showing Kingsley the eager hardness of her nipples.

"If you don't… God…if you don't move soon, you're going to kill me," he groaned out, his fingers flexing and curving around her waist, biting into her skin through the dress. His hips bucked up. Once. Kingsley muttered an apology, his face strained with self-control.

"Okay." She breathed out the word, matched his motion. "Oh!"

The pleasure made her vision go white, and she dug her nails into his chest. He gasped but didn't move. From the way he lay there, watching her while desire made him wet his lips and caused his breath to come faster, he planned on letting her do exactly what she wanted. Adah moved again, pressing down on him in a slow grind that stroked her deeply and sent fire racing through her. She moved faster. Tangled her fingers in his chest hair.

"God. Damn…" Kingsley bucked up into her and grasped her breasts through her dress, his thumb unerringly finding her nipples poking at the thin cloth.

A bolt of pleasure sizzled between Adah's nipples and the hot place between her thighs. She arched into his touch, snaked on top of him in search of more of the sweetness pouring through her body. She rode him faster, building the feeling, pushing the harsh sounds of her breath and his into the darkened room. The dress fell completely from her shoulders, and he gripped her exposed breasts, squeezed her nipples to pull her arousal higher and higher. It had been so long. So damn long.

The peak of her pleasure slammed into her, a sudden avalanche of feeling that dropped her down into him, crying out and gasping for breath. Her sweat-slick chest against his. Her heart galloped madly. Kingsley caught her, grabbed the back of her neck and brought her open mouth to his in a desperate and sloppy kiss. Then she was on her back, and he was rising over her, pushing her thighs even wider to expose where they were still joined. He pushed her dress up to her waist.

"My turn!" he breathed into her mouth.

He slammed into her, and she gasped at the sensation of him moving against her still-sensitive flesh, plunging into her again and again while she just held on, gripping his back, her neck arched. Adah cried out Kingsley's name. The sound of their sex was a liquid syncopation in the room as he took her again and again. And her desire rose again, swimming up to meet his.

"You feel so good," he groaned into her throat, his thrusts getting more erratic until he froze, buried at the deepest point inside her, spilling himself into the condom. She clenched her thighs against him, rubbing against him, wanting more.

He lifted his head, his eyes glittering and lips parted from his gasping breaths. "More?"

Mindless with want, she reached between them to touch herself. "Yes!"

Kingsley shoved her hand away and replaced it with his own, pulled out of her even though he was still hard. Her eyes rolled back in her head when he stroked her clitoris, slid what felt like three fingers into her clenching wetness.

"I have more," he growled.

Through the night, he gave and she took, then he took and she gave, an unending ouroboros of sex. When one was exhausted, the other took the reins and yoked pleasure around them again. The sheets dampened. The strip of condoms grew smaller. Every inch of Adah became almost too sensitive to touch, but she didn't want to stop. It was nearly dawn when Adah fell into an exhausted sleep on top of Kingsley, the two of them tangled together, the pillows tossed on the floor and room heady with the smell of their hard-won satisfaction.

Adah ached in the most wonderful way. She stretched in the soft sheets and felt the pull of muscles she hadn't used in years, the throb of bruises on her bare hips and her wrists where he'd held her down as he filled her over and over again with hard proof of his desire.

She rolled over in the bed, smiling around a moan of pleasure that slid past her lips. Faint sunlight from the bare window poured over her, warm and delicious, its tendrils sinking into her body with the sensation of a caress. Adah felt absolutely *amazing*. This intense physical satisfaction was something she could get used to, no matter how long it lasted. She opened her eyes to share the feeling with Kingsley. But she was alone in the bedroom.

Surprised, she sat up, and the sheets fell away to her waist, leaving her even more exposed to the blossoming sunrise. With her eyes fully open, she saw that her dress had been carefully folded and placed in the chair near the window, her purse on top of them, and her shoes tucked side by side on the floor.

She called Kingsley's name, once, then twice, but all she received in return was silence. No note rested on the bedside table. No smells of breakfast being made floated in from the kitchen. She frowned. The warmth she'd felt from their night of sensational sex began to fade. Quickly, she left the bed and got dressed.

After a quick exploration of the small house, she found the rest of it empty. No note. No idea of where he'd gone. Her first thought was to find him at the Hi-Winds Tournament. From what she remembered of the schedule, there was a men's kite-boarding race taking place that day, but it was in the afternoon. With the corner of her lip tucked between her teeth, she replayed the night before. The touches, the things they'd said to each other, what she may have said to him to scare him out of his own house.

All she remembered, though, was a passion-filled night and the hope for more before she went back home. No promises given or asked for. Just really, really good sex.

But on their after-dinner walk, Bennett had said something that haunted Adah now. *Men pay for sex with commitment and love¸ he'd told her. Women pay for love and commitment with sex. If he's like most guys in his situation, he probably thinks you want some sort of commitment from him to replace the one you're giving up with me.*

Adah had disagreed with him. Kingsley wasn't stupid enough to think something like that. She blinked and looked around the room, wondering. The longer she stood in the cold silence of the house, the more the words reverberated in her head. Did Kingsley really think she wanted that much more from him? The silence didn't give her another reason for his absence.

Okay then...

She fought the sharp stab of disappointment that he was the kind of coward to run away instead of telling her he didn't want more than a vacation screw. After washing her face and brushing her teeth with his toothpaste and her finger, she called a taxi and left his house the way she'd found it.

The taxi came quickly. The ride was unfortunately just long enough for her to replay everything that happened between her and Kingsley. The sex had been nothing short of amazing. The way he touched her, like he thought she was worthy of both lust and tenderness. He met her bite for bite, kiss for kiss, the fires of desire between them rising and falling through the night, only fully extinguishing when they both passed out from exhaustion.

Adah would have gladly loved to repeat the experience. But not if he was too much of a coward to tell her the limits of what she wanted and what he was willing to give.

She asked the driver to drop her off just short of the hotel. She walked the rest of the way and took a detour along the beach. The sun was rising still, and the island was faintly cool from the night's embrace. She shivered in her sundress and brushed her palms up her arms in a search for warmth.

Farther up the beach and just past her hotel, a group of people gathered in fluttering, semiformal clothes. A wedding. Or at least the end of one. Purple cloth, fine as gossamer, roped off an aisle leading to an arched arbor near the very edge of the beach and a few feet from the rush and retreat of the sea.

Nearly a dozen people gathered around a couple taking photographs while the purple cloth wavered in the early morning breeze. The wedding attendees all wore shades of yellow, and the bride and groom both wore white. The guests lifted full champagne flutes in the air and, after a toast that Adah couldn't hear, drank from their glasses before raining applause down on the newlyweds. Everyone looked happy.

Chapter 7

"Was it that good, or that bad?" Gage ashed his cigarette in the small saucer by his side.

Kingsley didn't say anything. He slumped down into the sand beside his friend and almost wished for a cigarette to clench between his teeth. What he really wanted to do was slip back into bed with Adah. It had been hell to leave her in the sheets that smelled like the two of them and were still warm from her body.

"Ah." Gage's teeth flashed in the low morning light. "You ran out on her like a little b—"

"No." Kingsley sighed. "Well, yes." He wasn't a strong believer in self-delusion.

He didn't know what he'd been thinking. Or

maybe that was it. He *hadn't* been thinking when he'd crawled out of bed and, after grabbing his clothes, out of the house. A walk through his neighborhood hadn't answered any of his questions, so it wasn't too long before he found himself on the comfortable stretch of beach where he and Gage occasionally swam, hosted parties, even slept on particularly debauched nights. And it hadn't been a surprise to see his friend awake and wandering the beach, smoking his habitual clove cigarette, hands shoved into the pockets of his cutoff shorts, his unbuttoned shirt blowing in the breeze.

Kingsley had wordlessly joined him, and they walked together toward the very edge of the beach, where the water flirted with their toes.

"So what's up with you and this chick, then? I thought you liked her."

Although Gage didn't hang around with Annika, Carlos and the rest, he knew just as much about what Kingsley got up to while on the island. They were good friends, not as tight as he was with his best friend, Victor, but nearly so.

"I *do* like her," Kingsley said. "That's the problem."

"Oh come on, dude." Gage blew out a stream of scented smoke. "Don't tell me you're one of those types who backs off as soon as the girl they're chasing shows some reciprocal interest."

"No, it's not that."

"Then what is it?"

It was a question Kingsley didn't want to answer. He liked Adah. He liked her to the point of distraction. She was beautiful, and sexy, and vulnerable even with her sharp edges. The problem was that after less than a week he liked her and enjoyed her company more than any other woman's. He wanted more of her. More time. More sex. More of everything. He was nervous about the sharp urgency of it all. But he was also nervous about something else.

"She was supposed to get engaged."

"I heard *was* in that sentence," Gage said.

"Yeah. She broke it off."

"Good. No problem. You can screw her guilt-free. I know you're one of those moral guys, all twisted about stuff like that."

Kingsley laughed. "Yeah. I typically think about right and wrong."

Although it *had* been a close thing with her warm and tempting in the hammock the night before when he knew all about the potential fiancé and still put his hand in her pants.

"She dumped him, and now she's probably looking to find a replacement. I'm not ready for that."

Gage drew on his cigarette, and the tip glowed hot in the low morning light. He blew the smoke toward the sky. "Did you ask her that mess, or just assume?"

"What else am I supposed to assume? She's at the age when most women get married. She just got rid of a fiancé out of necessity, and now she needs a replacement."

"You're assuming she's looking at this, at marriage, like a business arrangement. She's not the CEO of a billion-dollar business. From what you told me, she's not much of a businesswoman." He sucked on his cigarette again. "No shade, though."

Kingsley leaned forward to balance his elbows on his knees. His back twinged and his thighs burned, reminding him sharply of the night before, as if he even needed a reminder. Down on the beach, a couple in matching shorts and tank tops jogged past. He wondered vaguely if Adah was into things like that. Couples jogging. Matching outfits.

"Her parents need an investor to save their company. I looked into their business. It needs the help." Then he told his friend the whole story.

Gage narrowed his eyes, took his time sucking the last from the cigarette and ground down the butt into the white saucer between them.

"So, you're saying to me that you just had sex with a woman you've been calling all kinds of saint and gorgeous and everything else the last couple of days." Gage pinned him with a piercing stare. "You're talking about how she may be the one you've been looking for, and now that you got her into bed, now that she tossed aside this guy she's never even had sex with but promised herself to out of some crazy sense of family duty, now that she's done all that, you're saying she's some sort of a corporate gold digger using her body to get you to do what…?"

When Gage put it that way... "I'm not sure," Kingsley said. But his summary was accurate enough. He rubbed the back of his neck and cursed under his breath.

"You, my friend, are something else." Gage picked up the ashtray and stood up, the wind blowing his long curls away from his face. "Stay as long as you want. I gotta get ready for work." He walked away from Kingsley, taking the nearly hidden path toward his house far up on the beach.

With Gage gone, the sound of the wind seemed to pick up, rattling in Kingsley's ears like an accusation, taking up the slack where his friend left off.

Was he really that kind of guy? Kingsley stared at the peaking sun with the denials rising up in his mind. Of course, that's not what his actions meant. He wasn't looking for an excuse not to be with Adah now that she was free and could be with him as little or as much as he wanted. And he didn't want anything permanent. She was beautiful, and he was single. He just wanted some fun.

But maybe that was what she wanted, too? Gage's words rang in his ears again.

Kingsley let the sun rise over him, heating his body and bringing the sweat to the surface of his skin, warming to the point where he could smell himself, and smell Adah, too. He drew in a deep breath and took in all of it. His feelings, the sun, the lingering traces of her that clung to him like perfume.

He wanted to see her again. He wanted to touch her again. And as much as he was afraid of what *she* wanted, he was terrified of his own need that rose up in him every time he was around her.

Most nights, as he lay in bed and thought about her, it felt too intense to be real. A throbbing awareness that was more than sexual desire. More than simply enjoying the company of a beautiful woman. More intense than anything he'd ever experienced before.

With the sun free of the horizon and burning brightly in the sky like the realizations tumbling through his mind, he finally stood up and brushed off the bottom of his shorts. He drew a steadying breath and began to make his way home.

But when he got into the house, she wasn't there. Not that he could blame her. With no lover and no note, he could hardly expect her to just sit around and wait for him. Standing in the doorway of the bedroom that still smelled like their sex, he wanted nothing more than to have her back there again. In his arms. In his bed.

He needed to speak with her. He needed to see her.

After a quick shower and a change into presentable clothes—he didn't want to look like a complete bum if he ran into Adah's mother again—he drove to Adah's hotel. As he walked up to the front desk, he cursed under his breath, realizing he didn't know her last name.

As he walked up to the desk, he realized the woman there was vaguely familiar. Maybe she knew him enough to give him the information he wanted without him downright begging for it. He put on his most charming smile.

"Good morning, miss."

The woman looked up, smiling, from the stack of papers she'd been making notations on, a pen clasped between her fingers. Her smile disappeared when she saw Kingsley's face.

"Good morning, sir. May I help you?"

This was not his lucky day. The woman who looked back at him with a near scowl on her pretty face was one of the women who'd offered him the foursome days before. He'd assumed they were all tourists, but this was one of the girls who hadn't talked much. And even then, her Dutch accent had simply marked her as another visitor from the Netherlands enjoying the warmth of Aruba before going back to her European tundra. Faint malice stirred in her eyes.

Kingsley could see it was a lost cause, but he tried anyway. "I'd like to have one of your guests called, please."

Her eyes glinted. He could tell she wanted to say something about meeting him on the beach, maybe even about him leaving them high and dry at the hotel, but she pressed her lips together instead and shook her head. "Do you know this person's name or room number?"

"Her name is Adah." He looked her straight in the eyes. At least he knew her by more than just Doe Eyes now. Not that he'd get anywhere asking this particular woman for any information.

"And her last name?"

He clenched his teeth. "I don't know it." He might as well have just confessed to a one-night stand with a stranger. Someone he'd chosen over this woman and her two friends.

"Then I'm afraid I won't be able to help you." Her smile from earlier came back, pleased and sharp. "Sir."

He purposely kept his hands loose on top of the counter while he mentally searched for any clues to Adah's full name or how to get this woman to give up the room number, or at least call Adah and let her know he was down there waiting to see her. His eyes flicked up to the woman's hair, and its fall down her back despite the island heat. *Hair products.* Her family's business. An image of the jar his sister used on her hair nearly every day flashed in his mind.

"Mitchell," he said. "Adah Mitchell."

The smile fell away from the woman's face. With obvious reluctance, she typed something into the computer. When she finished whatever search she made, her sharp smile was back.

"I'm afraid we don't have an Adah Mitchell here," she said.

"Are you sure?" He resisted the urge to grab the

computer and yank it toward him so he could see for himself. "How about Adah Palmer?"

Just then another employee, this time a man, wearing a burgundy bow tie neatly tucked under the collar of his starched white shirt, appeared behind the desk.

"Excuse me, sir," Kingsley said. "Can you verify something for me?"

"Of course, I'll be more than happy to." After a puzzled look at his coworker, he sat in front of another computer station and tapped the mouse. "What can I do for you?"

The woman looked ready to throw something at him, but Kingsley was unbothered. He asked the young man about Adah.

"We don't have an Adah Mitchell or Palmer registered but we do have an Adah Palmer-Mitchell who checked out early this morning."

"Checked out? This morning?" It was barely eight o'clock.

"Yes, sir. She is no longer a guest with us."

Kingsley cursed under his breath. "All right. Thank you very much for your help." He turned to the woman, who still watched him with poison in her eyes. "And you, too."

He left the hotel and went back home, ignoring the alarm on his phone he'd set to remind him of his tournament later that morning. Online, he found out more about Adah Palmer-Mitchell than he'd known before. She lived in Atlanta and was the co-owner a fancy day care. Seeing photos of her on the computer only reinforced how far he was away from her, and what an idiot he'd been. Kingsley shut his laptop down and called his secretary.

Chapter 8

Kingsley glanced down at his phone when it vibrated for the third time in as many minutes.

Did you find the place OK?

Then:

Are you having trouble getting her? We put you on the list.

Then finally:

Let us know when you have her, OK?

He restrained himself from rolling his eyes, but just barely. His brother Wolfe had asked him to pick up his daughter from her Atlanta day care since he and his wife were stuck in a meeting that ran later than expected. It was only pure luck that Kingsley was even in town. Three weeks after leaving Aruba, he was still desperately searching for Adah. Every one of his online or phone leads had stopped at a dead end. Like she was being deliberately protected by someone or something. He stopped himself from outright hiring a private investigator. That would be creepy and strange. Instead, he'd taken a few days out of the office and flown to Atlanta himself, determined to find her the old-fashioned way.

So far he hadn't had any luck. But he was at least able to spend a day or so with his brother and sister-in-law, who were working an unexpectedly long-term business project in Atlanta. They'd been in the city for months and had their young daughter, Yasmine, with them.

And today, Wolfe had volunteered Kingsley to pick Yasmine up from day care.

Kingsley stuck his phone in the inside pocket of his blazer and climbed out of his rental SUV, opening the back door to check for the fifth or sixth time the stability of the car seat. He'd thought about using the day care's parking lot, but since he had to make a couple of phone calls before he got out, he didn't want to seem like a creep lurking in a place with children, especially a place where they didn't know him from Adam.

Kingsley shut and locked the car door with a chirp of the remote, then crossed the quiet street littered with pink summer blossoms from the trees swaying overhead. The music of children's voices rang up and down the tree-lined block.

The building in front of him was an attractive, two-story brick Georgian straight out of a fairy tale with kudzu clambering up its walls, and a small attic room framed in white perched on top of the roof. A low iron fence separated the wide front yard from the street, and a brick walkway led from the gate up to the short flight of steps and the wide porch.

He pressed the buzzer to the building, making sure to look straight into the camera he immediately noticed above the door.

"Good afternoon, sir." A warm voice greeted him after an electronic pulse. "How can I help you?"

"Good afternoon. I'm here to pick up Yasmine Diallo. I'm her uncle, Kingsley Diallo. Her parents should have my information on the appropriate list."

"One moment, sir."

The voice disappeared, then after about half a minute came back, welcoming him into the building.

The inside of Rosebud Academy was just as impressive as the outside, both professional and warm, with the person belonging to the voice on the other side of the intercom just a few feet from the door. A slim young man sat behind the desk, a laptop open in front of him that clearly showed a picture of Kingsley and a scanned copy of documents Kingsley couldn't make out from where he stood.

"Welcome to Rosebud Academy, sir."

"Thanks." He felt like he was about to pick up a stash of gold bricks. "What do I need to do now?"

"Yasmine is in her play session. It's almost over, so you can go there and pick her up." He gestured to a woman nearby Kingsley hadn't noticed before. "Mariah will escort you there."

In her low heels, black slacks and military-looking blouse, Mariah seemed official, welcoming *and* perfectly capable of kicking his ass if he so much as looked sideways at one of the kids. If he ever thought about enrolling any of his currently nonexistent kids into a day care of any kind, this was the type of place he'd want. He felt eyes on him at every step of the way, the setup of the school making it clear the welfare and safety of the children were top priorities.

Mariah walked beside Kingsley and made pleasant if forgettable conversation, guiding him down a brightly lit hallway with framed art on the walls. The air smelled faintly of lemons.

"Here we are." She stopped at a door leading outside, scanned a card attached to a lanyard around her neck and opened the door.

The backyard was another fairy tale. A high brick fence was decorated with colorful, wooden butterflies, snails and other creatures in large enough sizes for the kids to appreciate. The grass was lush and freshly cut, while swing sets and jungle gyms in miniature sat on one side of the large backyard next to a clearly marked area for hopscotch and jacks. Ten children who looked no older than three sat, ran and played on the spotless Astroturf in the center of the otherwise grassy yard. Everything was in perfect geometric order but still managed to convey a sense of warmth that the children seemed happy enough in.

Mariah pointed to Yasmine, but he'd already seen her. Tiny and coily-haired, she sat opposite another girl on the Astroturf, rolling an ambulance toward the girl's fire truck. They sat together, smiling and chatting in whatever common language they'd found while three women carefully watched the children, walking between them, sometimes stopping to ask questions or even playing with them.

A pair of legs stepped between Kingsley and his view of Yasmine and he tilted his head to glance around them and catch his niece's eye. But then something made him look up, heart suddenly beating triple time as he traced those bare feminine legs up to a close-fitting gray skirt and a pink blouse comfortable enough to wear in the summer heat, its collar loose around a slender throat. Adah's throat.

Unlike the version of her in Aruba, who had her hair in a ponytail or in thick waves down to her shoulders, this Adah wore her hair twisted to the crown of her head in a wispy bun with delicate tendrils floating around her face. She looked both professional and breathtakingly gorgeous.

Kingsley stared. The woman was in profile to him but it was unmistakably her. Smiling down at a boy who moments before had seemed on the verge of throwing a tantrum because neither of the girls nearby wanted to play with him. Kneeling down so she was at eye level, Adah soothed the boy with a touch and soon he was smiling back at her and showing her the toy train he'd discovered nearby.

Even though he'd been searching for Adah for nearly three weeks, all Kingsley could do was stare at her. It was like all his prayers had been answered in one heady rush. Kneeling only a few feet from Kingsley, she nodded and looked interested in everything the boy had to say, obviously encouraging him to show her how the toy train worked and distracting him from the tantrum he'd been working up to. Her face was gentle and smiling. She looked better than fine, even better than the last time Kingsley had seen her. In his bed.

The memory of her sleeping in his sheets shook him from his paralysis. He strode toward her, but his niece chose that moment to look up and, despite the fact that the woman he'd chased almost two thousand miles was kneeling temptingly close, he changed direction and headed toward Yasmine instead.

"Uncle King!" she gurgled softly and laughed, yanking at her playmate's sweater to point at Kingsley. "Uncle," she said again.

Adah stood up then, her eyes wide, a hand going to her waist. At first she stared at Kingsley like she

didn't recognize him. Then he remembered he was
wearing a suit, a bespoke Tom Ford that was just one
of many in his closet and part of his CEO uniform.
It was a *very* different outfit from the one he'd worn
the last time they'd seen each other. Granted, he'd
been naked at the time.

Before he reached Yasmine, Adah rushed over to
him, careful of the children scattered like so many
flower petals around her feet. She gripped his arm,
and he felt her touch through every layer of cloth,
smelled the unforgettable sweetness of her.

"What are you doing here?"

Before Kingsley could answer, Adah was dragging him away from Yasmine and toward the door
he'd stepped through with Mariah moments before.
Mariah, though she frowned in confusion, immediately stepped out onto the yard to take up watch
where Adah had been. Kingsley took a moment to
admire how efficient the place was run before he
allowed himself to be propelled through the door,
down the hallway with a click of Adah's heels and
into an office.

"What are you doing here?" she asked again. "You
can't be here."

Away from the children, her mask of control
dropped away. She dropped his arm and stepped all
the way across the room and behind her desk as soon
as they were behind the closed door together.

About to explain about his niece and the reason

he was at the day care, Kingsley frowned. "Why can't I be here?"

"The children…" she stuttered. "This is my life. I left you behind in Aruba." She stood up even straighter, her palms pressed against her belly while light from the wall of windows behind her haloed her rigid figure. "Just like you left me that morning."

Kingsley locked his muscles to hold off the tremors, a reaction to her words, he could feel gathering. This wasn't going to be an easy discussion. Not about him leaving her in bed that last morning, and definitely not about the reason he was in Atlanta searching for her. And though he'd put so much energy into finding her and trying to explain, now he was simply tongue-tied and didn't know what to say to make her listen to him.

"I'm sorry." That was a decent start.

But she didn't seem impressed. "That's what you came here for? That could have been an email. That could have been something you said to your priest and kept it moving."

He winced. It wasn't like he didn't deserve her scorn, though. "I was an idiot," he said. "I made some assumptions and acted on them without even talking with you." He was too embarrassed to say what those assumptions were. But her face said he didn't have to. His cowardly behavior that morning said plainly what he'd been afraid of.

"I wasn't ready to be anyone's fiancé." He said the words out loud anyway, just to get his stupidity out there. "That's what I thought that morning. That's why I ran."

Just like Kingsley thought, he wasn't telling her anything she hadn't thought of herself. "And now you're here, do you still think that?" Adah shifted, arms crossing over her chest, her feet planted wide.

Before he could answer, a knock sounded on the door. Adah looked toward it and raised her voice.

"Yes?"

"It's getting late, Adah. Perhaps Mr. Diallo needs to make an appointment to speak with you at another time when it's not so close to dismissal." It was Mariah on the other side of the door, as levelheaded as Kingsley expected her to be, brief though their acquaintance had been.

"We'll only be a few more moments, Mariah. I promise not to let him kidnap any of the children on his way out."

The dead silence from the other side of the door gave Kingsley an idea just how funny Mariah thought that comment was.

"I only came to take one child with me," he said raising his voice so the woman on the other side of the door could hear him. "I don't want Mariah to gut me based on your bad jokes."

"I'll tell Yasmine you'll be out here shortly," Mariah called back to him the same moment Adah drew a sharp breath and slapped her palms down on the desk as if to brace herself against a blow. The fading sound of Mariah's practical shoes against the floor dominated the brief silence.

"You have a child here?" Adah asked softly, her tone making it clear that she'd not only felt betrayed by him in Aruba, but expected the same treatment from him here, as well.

"My niece is here," he rushed to explain. "Yasmine Diallo."

"Oh." Her face softened just the tiniest bit. The hydraulic chair behind the desk hissed softly as she sat down. "She's beautiful."

"Yes, she is. Beautiful babies do tend to run in our family."

"Not to boast or anything?" Adah raised her brows in question and leaned back in the chair. She looked, suddenly, exhausted. Outside when he'd first seen her, she'd looked even better than the last time they were together. Now that they were away from the chaos of the children and the distractions of other people, he saw the signs of skillfully applied makeup, a slight puffiness around her eyes. She looked stressed.

"How is your mother?" he asked. "Did she let you out of the agreement without any trouble?"

"She did, actually." A faint smile touched her face. "It was all so much easier than I thought. It hasn't taken her long to come to terms with my decision. She's almost happier now."

"Good."

Silence, broken only by the faint hum of the air

conditioner, closed in on them. The wall of windows behind her looked out onto the backyard with the children, but the glass was visibly tinted, allowing light in, but not unwelcome eyes.

Kingsley felt awkward looming above Adah in her own office. He sat in the chair across from her desk and shifted to be as comfortable as he could in an uncomfortable situation. "Do you regret it?" he asked her.

"Regret what?"

"Any of it."

Adah sighed again and dipped her head to stare thoughtfully at the neatly arranged surface of her desk while Kingsley watched her every move. His belly clenched tight, he prepared himself for her to say she regretted meeting him and hated the night they spent together.

She lifted her head and met his gaze. "No. I don't."

If Kingsley had any doubts he was doing the right thing by chasing Adah to the other side of her world, they all vanished with that one look. He'd pursued her, seduced her from her promises to another man, then run off like a coward and a fool once she ended up in his bed. Still, she didn't hate him.

Here, in her everyday life, she was as lovely as she'd been under the Aruban moonlight. Seductively sweet with her plush mouth and angular cheeks. Compelling from him the desire to make her smile, make her respond to him, make her stay. This wasn't just about vacation sex. On the island, it had actually scared him how much he felt for her. He wasn't scared anymore.

"Will you have dinner with me tonight?"

The mask of indifference fell back over her face, and she stiffened. "Why?"

"Because I've missed you." It felt freeing to say the words.

"How can you miss someone you never had?" she asked.

"I never had you, but I shared your company, and I thought we enjoyed each other."

She shook her head, the mask slipping when she bit the corner of her mouth.

Something terrible suddenly occurred to him, and he sat up in the chair. "Are you seeing someone?"

"No!" She looked like he'd just accused her of murder. "You came into this place by complete happenstance. You didn't know I work here. I just… I don't want you to ask me out because you think it's what I want. I'm not going to force you to pretend you want to still fool around with me just because the world is a small place." Adah drew a breath, looking everywhere but at Kingsley's face. "We slept together, and it's really no big deal."

"It is a big deal to *me*," he said, very carefully weighing his next words. "Sure, I stumbled into you here by pure dumb luck, but I've been searching all over the place. Online, off-line, everything. I searched so much that it felt like you were trying to hide from me."

"I..." Her eyes flickered wide in surprise as she seemed to take in what he just said. "I'm not into the social media thing and the business is listed as an LLC."

"That explains it. I guess I'll have to get to know you properly the old-fashioned way."

"The 'old-fashioned way'?" she asked softly. "That's a little too late for us—don't you think?"

The memory of their night together flared abruptly to life in Kingsley and he had to clench every muscle in his body before his reaction became too obvious. He cleared his throat.

"Nothing is too late for us," he said. "Have dinner with me and we can start over, do things the right way." He paused, wanting desperately for her to say yes. But he didn't want to look too eager either. "So...is that a yes?"

She breathed a gentle laugh. "Okay."

"Tonight?"

Adah laughed again. "Tonight."

"Seven o'clock?"

"Let's do eight instead," she said. "I have a few things to take care of first."

She gave him her home address, and he tried to play it cool as he typed it into his phone. But he was pretty sure she saw his hands trembling. After he'd gathered Yasmine in the car seat and taken her to Wolfe and Nichelle's rented condo, amused and fed her until they showed up nearly two hours later, he realized he didn't want to wait until dinnertime to see Adah again. It was at least another two hours away. He'd searched for her for nearly three weeks. Another two hours was too long for him to wait.

So as soon as Wolfe and Nichelle were settled in with their daughter, he left and went back to the day care. When he got there, only two cars waited in the parking lot. He pressed the buzzer on the porch's intercom system and waited. And waited. He was about to turn away and head back to his car when the intercom crackled to life. Her voice sounded through the electronic box and he smiled in relief.

"You know we're closed." But there was warmth in her words.

"Yes, but I figured you'd make an exception for me."

"You're very cocky," she said as the door released with a soft electronic chime.

"You would know," he said the last under his breath, and he slipped through the door, making sure it closed and locked firmly behind him.

Without bothering to ask where she was, he followed his memory to her office where he found her seated behind her desk and watching the door expectantly.

"I wasn't going to cancel on you tonight," she said.

"I know." He closed her door and leaned back against it, shoving his hands in his pockets. "I didn't want to wait," he said.

Adah looked at her watch. "Dinner is less than two hours from now. Are you that impatient?" But there was a flare of something in her eyes, something that matched the answering fire low in his belly.

"Yes, I am." He finally gave up his nonchalant pose by the door and crossed to her desk while she watched him with a fraction of the hunger he felt building inside him.

"I really did look for you everywhere," he said. "I bribed people to tell me where you lived. I think I even called in a favor from an old girlfriend who works at the DMV. Nobody would tell me anything about you."

He leaned on her desk, his palms flat on its surface in a mirror of the pose she had taken when facing him earlier that day. The desk felt cool under his hands, his own body well on its way toward overheating.

"Whatever you want to know, all you have to do is ask me." She leaned back in her chair and smiled serenely up at him.

"Will you marry me?" The words tumbled up out of his hot throat.

"What?" Her serenity disappeared. She shoved back from the desk with the explosion of sound, looking at him like he was crazy. Maybe he *was* crazy.

Kingsley swallowed convulsively, shocked at himself. He wasn't an impulsive man. Not by any means, but this… He opened his mouth to take the words back but immediately realized he didn't want to.

It wasn't his fear of Adah asking too much that

had made him run; it was because he wanted her so immediately and completely in his life that it frightened him. His own desires, raw and unfamiliar, for one woman and one woman alone had made him question everything. From fear of the unrelenting firing squad of those questions, he'd simply pulled on his running shoes and fled like his very life depended on it.

He didn't need to run anymore.

"Will you marry me, Adah Palmer-Mitchell? I want you in my life. I want to snorkel with you and make love with you all night, then breakfast in the morning. I want to share *everything* with you. Will you have me?"

"I...I don't know. This is a little soon, isn't it?" She stared at him, her eyelashes fluttering in agitation.

Was it too soon to know whether or not you wanted to spend the rest of your life with someone who made your pulse race, your heart soar and your moods light? Kingsley knew at some point, it could be too *late*, and he didn't want that.

He knew he was acting impulsively, but he also knew he was doing the right thing. With her wide eyes firmly on him, Adah stood up from behind the desk, a slow rising to her feet that revealed to him again the sweetly slender form, her hips clad in the gray skirt still somehow managing to be alluring despite its conservative shade. She watched him as if she expected him to flinch back and run like a startled animal.

"Ask me again." She rounded the desk, her footsteps soundless on the thin carpet.

He asked without hesitation.

"Okay." She reached his side of the desk, her scent of ginger and sugar undoing him breath by breath. "If you're still in Atlanta in the morning, I'll give you a proper answer."

Kingsley moved even closer to her, breathing her in after an absence that had nearly torn him apart. Her answer wasn't exactly the one he wanted, but he could work with it. For now, her breath and her presence were enough.

"Can I still see you tonight?" he asked, every breath he took spiced by her sweet scent.

Adah pressed her lips together, her eyes darting down his body, then away. She sighed, the look on her face one he recognized as the one she wore when she was accusing herself of doing or saying something stupid.

"I... Yes." With a delicate twist of her body that brought Kingsley's eyes skimming her waist and hips, she turned away to grab a notepad from her desk and scribble something on it. "This is my phone number. Call if you're going to be late."

He took the note like it was a lifeline. "I won't be late."

"Good. See you then."

Chapter 9

At 6:53 p.m., Adah clutched her cell phone and told her mother that no, she didn't need to come over. But Thandie Palmer-Mitchell could ignore her child like a pro, and within thirty minutes, she appeared at Adah's front door with a bottle of red wine and a bowl of sliced fruit.

"I have some deconstructed sangria." She held up the bottle and fruit as she walked past Adah and into the apartment. "You can tell me what's wrong while we put this thing together." She dropped her purse and scarf on the couch, then looked searchingly at Adah. "I heard something strange in your voice earlier so don't waste your breath telling me nothing is wrong."

Ever since Aruba and the broken pre-engagement, her mother had been even more attentive than usual. Adah was consumed with panic and fear about disappointing her parents, and was sure her mother sensed those emotions.

"Mother… Mama, everything is fine. I just had a little surprise today—that's all. Nothing to worry about," Adah said.

But Kingsley showing up at her workplace in his designer suit had been more than a *little* surprise. He looked like a completely different person away from the sea and the tropical sun, his unforgettable body clothed in a tailored suit. But the look in his eyes had been the same. Alternate hunger and amusement. Like he wanted to both devour her and laugh with her. Maybe both at the same time.

Adah shivered at the thought, then glanced at her watch. How long did her mother plan on being here?

After the first *and* last time her mother and Kingsley met, Adah wasn't eager for the two of them to see each other again. At least not until she was certain where she and Kingsley stood. He said he was done running. But lip service was something Adah was very familiar with. After all, she'd been giving her mother plenty of it over the years when it came to her proposed marriage with Bennett. Adah sighed and reluctantly followed her mother into the kitchen.

"Mama, I promise you I'm okay." She stopped herself from looking at her watch, knowing damn well she only had about twenty minutes until Kingsley showed up. If he was the punctual type.

"I don't believe you, darling." Her mother was pouring the wine over the fruit in a punch bowl. "I don't want you to feel alone in whatever you're going through. I made you a promise, and I intend to keep it."

Adah smiled, warmed by her mother's words. It meant everything that they'd come out on the other end of the marriage disaster with their relationship stronger than before. But she also didn't want it all to implode when Kingsley showed up at her doorstep.

Her mother had taken the broken potential engagement better than Adah thought she would. It also helped that less than a week later, a billion-dollar beauty corporation even Adah had heard of made her parents an offer of partnership with Palmer-Mitchell Naturals that had the family celebrating for days.

"Now we just need to let this soak for about an hour or so while we talk." Her mother looked so pleased with herself that Adah didn't have the heart to throw her out.

She nibbled on her bottom lip despite the lipstick she'd freshened up a few minutes before. "In that case, there's something I need to—" The doorbell rang, cutting her off.

Her mother frowned. "Are you expecting someone else, darling?"

I wasn't expecting you, Adah thought. But she bit her tongue and threw a glance toward the front door, then back to her mother. "I invited a friend over," she said, making her way toward the door.

"A *friend*?" Her mother braced her palms on top of the kitchen counter, frown firmly in place. There was no way she'd misinterpreted what kind of friend Adah had invited to her apartment. "So soon?"

Adah blushed and turned away, alternately wanting to placate her mother and needing to invite Kingsley in so he wouldn't disappear again. "He's actually someone I knew from before."

Her mother followed her from the kitchen, her high heels tapping against the hardwood floors like the sound of a telltale heart, which only made Adah's actual heart beat faster in nervousness and dread. She drew a breath and pulled open the door.

Of course it was Kingsley. And he looked…

Her heartbeat raced in her chest, but this time the reason for it was completely different. Even with her mother behind her, Adah couldn't stop her body from responding to him. He'd changed into another three-piece suit. This one was a dark gray with a tie and pocket square the same gold as his skin. The vest accentuated his flat belly, and she dropped her eyes immediately to where it parted in an inverted V just above his crotch. Adah licked her lips and swallowed.

"I'm a little early," he said, his voice a deep bass settling hard in her belly.

If her mother hadn't been in the room, Adah would have dragged him into her apartment and jumped him. Maybe it was a good thing her mother was there after all. In lieu of doing what she really wanted, she devoured his gorgeous body with her eyes.

"Adah, aren't you going to introduce us?"

Kingsley looked over her shoulder at her mother's words, and Adah forced her mind to focus.

"Um…come in." She stepped back to invite him inside. To Thandie she said, "You've met him before. At the hotel in Aruba."

Her mother drew in a shocked breath. She started to speak the same time Kingsley said, "If this is a bad time, I can come back."

"No!" Adah practically shouted. She ignored her mother's surprise, and half hoped she would allow him the same courtesy she'd shown Bennett when he showed up at her door in Aruba. But no such luck. Instead her mother stepped forward with her hand extended.

"I'm Thandie Palmer-Mitchell," she said. "And you are?"

Adah squeezed her eyes shut in embarrassment. "Mother…"

But Kingsley was already stepping forward to shake her mother's hand. "Kingsley Diallo, ma'am. I'm interested in marrying your daughter."

The resulting silence didn't last long.

"Why only *interested*?" Her mother glanced up at Kingsley with her arms crossed. From the look on her face, she might as well have been looking down at him. Kingsley didn't seem the least bit intimidated.

Instead, he stood respectfully quiet, nodding once at the loaded question.

"Because your daughter hasn't told me yes."

Her mother made a show of examining Kingsley from head to toe. The frown she'd been wearing deepened even more. "I know you," she said.

"Mama, I already told you. You met him at the hotel in Aruba. He just has more clothes on." Adah bit her tongue after she said the last part, wondering what the hell was wrong with her.

"No, there's something else…" Her mother's eyes widened, and a hand went to her throat. If she'd been wearing pearls, Adah swore she would have clutched them. "Are you one of the Miami Diallos?"

"I am, ma'am." Kingsley said it calmly while Adah was the one to frown now. What did where he lived have to do with anything?

"Oh." Her mother looked shell-shocked.

"Mama? Are you okay?" Adah stared at her mother, then at Kingsley, confused.

"Yes, love," her mother said, but she still looked like she'd just received the surprise of her life. "I'm going to leave you to your…whatever it is you and Mr. Diallo have planned for tonight. You can have the sangria anytime you like." Then she was gathering her purse and scarf from where she'd dropped them on the couch. "We'll talk later." She nodded at Kingsley. "Let me know how your proposal goes."

He smiled. "I will, ma'am."

Once her mother pulled the front door shut behind her, Adah turned to Kingsley. "What was that about?"

"A business proposition my company presented to her last week. Nothing you have to worry about."

But Adah couldn't let it go so easily. "Wait a minute. You're from the Diallo Corporation?"

He nodded. "Is that going to be a problem for you?"

"But…but…" She couldn't even think of a proper objection. He'd basically saved her parents' business, no, her *family's* business. Because of his connection with her.

"It was business," he said with a shrug, walking toward her with a compelling and graceful movement of hips that made her mouth water. "It makes sense to us. You brought Palmer-Mitchell Naturals to my attention, but after talking it over with the board, they agree the partnership makes good business sense."

"Oh." Adah felt like she was losing the basic ability to speak.

"Now, about you and me…" A lopsided smile tugged at his sinful mouth and took whatever else was left of Adah's reasoning abilities.

She stayed right where she was while he stalked toward her. "What about you and me?" The words didn't leave her mouth above a whisper.

Earlier when he'd asked her that ridiculous question, she'd been shocked. This from the man who ran from the passionate bed they'd shared as if it were on fire. It didn't make any sense. She'd just left one engagement behind, for God's sake.

But between the moment he'd left her at the day care and when he appeared at her front door, she'd relived what it had been like without him over the last few weeks. Not just the sex she'd ached for, even though it had been unforgettably good. But the way he'd brought his own light into her life. His fearlessness, his humor, his strength. It didn't matter he was suddenly a millionaire or billionaire able to be the savior to Palmer-Mitchell Naturals her parents wanted. He was what *she* wanted.

"Be with me." His breath whispered against her lips. "However you want to do this, just be with me."

His words rang through her, resonating with every desire she'd ever had. "Yes," Adah said while the feeling rose up inside her like the sun-washed tides of an unforgettable Aruban sea. "Always, yes."

She met his lips halfway and allowed his desire, and hers, to sweep her completely away.

* * * * *

SPECIAL EXCERPT FROM

HARLEQUIN

KIMANI ROMANCE

*After scoring phenomenal success in Phoenix with
her organic food co-op, Naomi Stallion is ready to
introduce Vitally Vegan to her Utah town. But a nasty
bidding war over the property Naomi wants to buy
pits the unconventional lifestyle coach against sexy,
überconservative corporate attorney Patrick O'Brien.
When the stakes rise, will Patrick choose his career or the
woman he yearns for?*

*Read on for a sneak peek at
SWEET STALLION,
the next exciting installment in author
Deborah Fletcher Mello's **THE STALLIONS** series!*

Naomi shifted her gaze back to the stranger's, her palm
sliding against his as he shook her hand. The touch was
like silk gliding across her flesh, and she mused that he had
probably never done a day's worth of hard labor in his life.
"It's nice to meet you, Patrick," she answered. "How can
we help you?"

"I heard you mention the property next door. Do you
mind sharing what you know about it?"

She looked him up and down, her mind's eye assembling
a photographic journal for her to muse over later. His eyes
were hazel, the rich shade flecked with hints of gold and
green. He was tall and solid, his broad chest and thick arms
pulling the fabric of his shirt taut. His jeans fit comfortably

KPEXP0817

against a very high and round behind, and he had big feet. Very big feet in expensive, steel-toed work boots. He exuded sex appeal like a beacon. She hadn't missed the looks he was getting from the few women around them, one of whom was openly staring at him as they stood there chatting.

"What would you like to know about Norris Farms?" Naomi asked. She crossed her arms over her chest, the gesture drawing attention to the curve of her cleavage.

Patrick's smile widened. "Norris," he repeated. "That's an interesting name. Is it a fully functioning farm?"

"It is. They use ecologically based production systems to produce their foods and fibers. They are certified organic."

"Is there a homestead?"

"There is."

"Have the owners had it long? Is there any family history attached to it?"

Naomi hesitated for a brief second. "May I ask why you're so interested? Are you thinking about bidding on this property?"

Patrick clasped his hands behind his back and widened his stance a bit. "I'm actually an attorney. I represent the Perry Group and they're interested in acquiring this lot."

Both Naomi and Noah bristled slightly, exchanging a quick look.

Naomi scoffed, apparent attitude evident in her voice. "The Perry Group?"

Patrick nodded. "Yes. They're a locally owned investment company. Very well established, aren't they?"

Her eyes narrowed as she snapped, "We know who they are."

Don't miss SWEET STALLION
by Deborah Fletcher Mello, available September 2017
wherever Harlequin® Kimani Romance™
books and ebooks are sold!

Get 2 Free Books,
Plus 2 Free Gifts—
just for trying the
Reader Service!

KIMANI™ ROMANCE